KU-427-368

THE "DARK SECRET"

BLACKIE & SON LIMITED
16/18 William IV Street, Charing Cross, LONDON, W.C.2
17 Stanhope Street, GLASGOW

BLACKIE & SON (INDIA) LIMITED
103/5 Fort Street, BOMBAY

BLACKIE & SON (CANADA) LIMITED
TORONTO

G 715

DISASTER TO THE "VENTURE"

Page 36

Frontispiece

THE "DARK SECRET"

BY

PERCY F. WESTERMAN

Author of "The Missing Diplomat" "Contraband" &c.

Illustrated by

VICTOR J. BERTOGLIO

BLACKIE & SON LIMITED
LONDON AND GLASGOW

Printed in Great Britain by Blackie & Son, Ltd., Glasgow

CONTENTS

ILLUSTRATIONS

THE "DARK SECRET"

CHAPTER I — CAUGHT OUT

There were a dozen reasons why the *Venture*, manned by the Seagull Patrol of the 1st Otherport Sea Scouts, should not be out there in the teeth of a rapidly rising gale. Some they knew; others they did not, which, in the circumstances, was all to the good.

They were without their Scoutmaster and in consequence ought not to be outside the limits of the port, even though Ron Bradley, the P.L., was almost as capable of handling a boat as was the Skipper, as Mr. Dyson was called.

Unfortunately the S.M. had been rushed to hospital, for an urgent operation, on the previous day. The *Venture* had been left at Nigel Cove, fifteen miles to the west'ard of her home port, and it was out of the question to leave her there, at the mercy of 'longshore thieves and on-shore gales, until Mr. Dyson was fit again.

The *Venture* was the pride and joy of the

1st Otherport Sea Scouts. Originally a naval pinnace, she had passed through various owners' hands, and in due course had been fitted with a car engine of ancient vintage that was supposed to develop 12 horse-power.

By dint of hard work and careful saving the Troop had managed to raise the purchase price, namely thirty-five pounds. What an advance she was on the Montague whaler, that depended for propulsion upon six ash oars or a modest sail area: with the new craft there would be no question of whether there was a breeze or not!

"Sound?" echoed the watery-eyed individual who was disposing of the craft. "'Course she is! She's teak built, ain't she, and teak'll last you fellows out. If you doubt my word, just you watch while I sticks me knife in her."

He suited the action to the words, inserting the point of the blade into the boat's sides in half a dozen places.

"She seems all right," conceded the Scoutmaster.

"Seems? Naturally! Teak's the only wood as'll keep its natural oil in fresh or salt water. Oak isn't much good in fresh water and elm's a jolly sight worse! There you are, mister; take her or leave her. It's all the same to me!"

That was two months ago. Since then the

Sea Scouts had put to sea in the *Venture* on many occasions. They had discovered slight defects and had managed to put them right. They had dismantled and overhauled the engine so that, instead of displaying its former habit of giving up the ghost at inopportune moments, the motor could be relied upon to keep chugging along in a manner that imparted a sense of reliability to the *Venture's* youthful crew.

And the crew? Scoutmaster Dyson, popularly known as the Skipper, was out of it owing to unfortunate circumstances beyond his control.

The Patrol-leader, Ronald Bradley, was a tall, well set up youth of seventeen who had the sea in his blood as had his father and grandfather before him, and even further back, if one believes the stories told in Otherport of " them Bradleys ".

Ned Henderson was the Second. Although of an impulsive nature he was shaping well. There was very little of the " look before you leap " in his composition, and the lack of it was apt to lead him into trouble at times.

Tom Moore, usually known as Christie, and Jim Coleman, who answered readily enough to Musty, were the most mechanical-minded members of the crew. It was upon them that the duties of engineer fell lightly and to their great satisfaction. What they couldn't coax out of the *Venture's* motor no professional mechanic in Otherport could.

Then there was Georgie Hughes, otherwise " Cookie ", whose deficiencies in the art of seamanship were counter-balanced by a genuine interest in the galley. He believed in the maxim, " a well-fed ship is a happy ship ", and it was evident that when there was grub on board Cookie would always be on time when an appetizing and satisfying meal became due.

Mervyn Long, otherwise Lofty, was the signalling expert. Although all the crew had been trained in semaphore and Morse, Lofty outshone them all. There, again, the gift might have been hereditary, since his father was a Signal Boatswain, R.N., now retired. In addition, Lofty was an adept at knotting and splicing, and much of the *Venture's* standing and running gear bore evidence of his skill in this direction. There was never a frayed rope's end on board. Spanish pennants, as they are called, were Lofty's pet abomination.

Finally the tenderfoot, Wee Jock Anderson, red-haired and cheeky-faced. He had only recently been promoted from the Cubs, and the story went that the Akela shed tears at his departure; whether of joy and relief or of regret, the Troop didn't know. Already his mischievousness on board had been decidedly

With Henderson at the wheel—and it wanted a fairly hefty youth to steer through that lump of breaking seas—Roy was able to go below and look round.

The rest of the crew, with the exception of Musty, who was refilling a grease cap, were cheerful enough. In fine weather they would have been in the cockpit; but for some unexplained reason, they preferred to fug in the little cabin in an atmosphere composed largely of oil fumes from the engine.

Georgie Hughes was squatting within a foot or two of a roaring Primus stove and holding on to an iron dixie, the smell from the contents of which acted as a foil to the reek of the engine.

"How goes it, George?"

"Fine!" replied the cook. "Grub'll be ready in half an hour."

"Good!" rejoined the Patrol-leader. "Give Wee Jock a hand with the pump, Lofty!"

"Is she leaking?" asked Long.

"No fear! Only a lot of spray coming inboard."

In his own mind Ron wasn't so sure about it. The amount of water sluicing under the floorboards could hardly be accounted for in the way he had suggested. But another thing he felt fairly certain about; and that was that the crew weren't likely to enjoy that stew!

A nasty cross sea sent the Patrol-leader hard against the door frame as he emerged from the cabin. The *Venture* was in the thick of it. If the motor failed now . . .

A glance on the port beam showed the headland more than a mile away, with spray being thrown up almost to its summit, which was nearly two hundred feet above sea-level. Close to the edge of the cliff was a small wooden hut, and in that hut Ron knew there would be two of the 1st Otherport Sea Scouts keeping watch.

Two of the Kittiwake patrol were on duty up there. Who they were, Bradley did not know; but they were keeping an eye on the battling *Venture*, although what they could do if anything befell her was a debatable problem. In the event of a breakdown of the engine, anything might happen before the coast watchers could telephone for the Otherport lifeboat to put out to the rescue.

"I wish we were safely out of it," thought the Patrol-leader, conscious of an indescribable parched sensation in his throat. It wasn't on his own account he had expressed the wish; it was the thought that he was responsible for the safety of the crew. They had still a considerable distance to go and the wind was steadily increasing.

For quite ten minutes Lofty and Wee Jock took turns at the bilge pump. Somehow the amount of water under the stern-grating did not appear to be diminishing.

Lifting up the grating, Ron examined the stern-tube, which was momentarily submerged every ten seconds or so as the *Venture* rose on the crest of a wave. Gingerly, to avoid having his fingers caught by the rapidly revolving shaft, he tested the grease-cap and gave it a couple of turns. As he did so he noticed that as the little craft lifted her stern to the seas there was quite a nasty gush of water close to the gland.

That was nothing much to worry about. It meant merely tightening a couple of nuts to force the metal collar farther into the stern-tube.

"Bring a spanner along, Christie!" ordered the Patrol-leader. "Stern-gland's leaking a bit."

Tom Moore emerged, knelt down and adjusted the spanner to one of the nuts.

"She's tight already!" he declared. "My word! It is coming in, but not through the gland."

"Then where?" asked Ron.

Christie did not reply at once. He was engaged in doing something with the spanner, and his back obstructed the Patrol-leader's view.

"Gosh!" he exclaimed at length. "It's the whole of the stern-tube working loose!"

"Can't you do anything?"

"Might," replied Tom dubiously. "Don't like messing about with it too much. The whole thing might come adrift and then we'd be properly in the soup! Just you look!"

He stood aside to let Ron examine the defect. Without a doubt water was pouring in through the hole in the deadwood through which the stern-tube passed. Two coach-screws holding down the flange had rusted right through.

Obviously repairs could not be effected without drawing the threaded parts of the screws, and that was a task beyond the resources of the crew while the *Venture* was afloat.

"We'll have to carry on and trust to luck, Ron," declared Tom. "I'll get Musty to slow her down a bit. That'll lessen the vibration!"

Mishaps at sea rarely come alone.

Almost before Christie had finished speaking, a heavy cross sea hit the *Venture* on the port beam. Instead of pitching, she heeled.

There was a crash below, followed by clouds of steam from the cabin.

"What's up now?" asked the Patrol-leader.

"Dixie capsized!" replied Lofty.

"Anyone scalded?"

"No fears! Worse than that—our dinner's gone west."

"Then tighten your belts and make the best of it!" rejoined the Patrol-leader. "And one of you had better get busy with a bucket."

"What's wrong with the pump?" asked Hughes.

"Nothing! Only it happens it isn't man enough for the job. Get busy, there!"

" Couldn't bring her up in time to meet it!" declared Ned. " A brute of a cross sea—and here's another! Up, my beauty!"

He put the helm up to bring the bow on to a particularly vicious sea.

For a few moments the *Venture* seemed to be standing on her heel; then, as the wave passed harmlessly underneath, she slid down the reverse side, bringing her bows under a solid mass of water.

Like a submarine emerging, her fore-part reappeared, shedding water in a double cascade.

" Fine!" shouted Henderson. " She'll live through anything!"

" Good for you, Ned!" bawled Ron in reply. " Watch the big 'uns!"

It was one thing—and a consoling thought—to know that the little craft was able to ride the menacing seas; another, to realize that she was leaking badly and that only by combined effort was the inrush kept under control.

Then came the rain: heavy downpours

between periods of misty drizzle. This was all to the good up to a certain point. It beat down the vicious crests. On the other hand, visibility was at times restricted to less than a quarter of a mile. The shore was entirely blotted out, so that a compass course had to be followed.

Presently Ron, who had relieved the Second at the wheel, beckoned to him.

"Keep your eyes skinned for the West Rat's Tail buoy, Ned! It should be on our port bow unless we've overrun it in this misty rain."

Through his binoculars Henderson searched the blurred horizon. It was imperative to sight the buoy, one that had to be passed before making an eight-point turn to port and so bringing the *Venture* to the first pair of fairway buoys leading to Otherport Harbour.

If the West Rat's Tail were missed in the rain, there was danger of the *Venture* running upon the Whelps, an extended ledge of half-tide rocks where, once a craft strikes hard, she rarely if ever gets off.

"See anything?" asked the Patrol-leader.

"Yes! Almost dead ahead! It's not the buoy, though. It's a small craft of some sort. Port a bit! At that! You're right on it!"

"I see her!" declared Ron after a while. "What's she doing out here? Looks as if she's anchored."

"It's no place to bring up on a day like

this," rejoined Ned, raising his glasses and focusing them on the little craft again. "Why, she's a yacht—dismasted! My error! She isn't; but she's flying a signal of sorts!"

"On deck, Lofty!" bawled the Patrol-leader. "There's a yacht making a signal!"

The announcement brought not only Lofty Long, but the rest of the crew who had been sheltering in the cabin. Jimmy and Wee Jock, who had again taken a spell at the baling operations, desisted to see what was happening until they were ordered to stick to their job.

Rapidly the distance between the *Venture* and the stranger decreased, for the seas, though high, were not so menacing and the wind had eased slightly.

The yacht proved to be of about five or six tons, sloop rigged with a Bermudan mast. Apparently the single halliard for hoisting the mainsail had parted, for the canvas, still held in the metal track, was bunched untidily on deck. The staysail, too, was loosely stowed, and the yacht was riding, not to her own ground tackle, but to a sea-anchor.

From her masthead two flags streamed out-board—hard in the strong wind. On the *Venture's* present bearing they appeared end-on so that they could not be distinguished. Just above the after end of the low coach roof could be seen the sou'wester of one of the crew.

"Can you make out the signal, Lofty?" asked the Patrol-leader. "Take Ned's glasses."

"I could read them if they weren't blowing out towards us," declared Long. "We'll have to wait till we're more abeam. Edge her to starboard a bit, Ron!"

Soon the two flags became distinguishable: the upper one with five horizontal stripes, blue, white, red, white and blue—the other chequered blue and white like part of a chess board.

Every member of the *Venture's* crew, including Wee Jock Anderson, knew what that two-flag hoist signified. Any mariner, of whatever nationality, could read and understand its grim significance.

In the Esperanto of the Seven Seas it read "N.C.". Translated into English it meant: "In distress; need immediate assistance."

It was an appeal to which no seaman would turn a deaf ear or a blind eye. No matter the hazard, the attempt must be made; otherwise, the master of the craft refusing aid would be branded as a coward and unworthy of the glorious traditions of the sea.

"Stand by, Musty!" ordered the Patrol-leader. "Be ready to put her into reverse or to stop her directly I give the word. Out fenders! We may have to run alongside her."

In his mind Ron hoped that such a step would not be necessary. In this sea there would be the imminent danger of the two craft rolling together, to their common destruction; or the *Venture*, carrying too much way, might overshoot the sloop and get her propeller fouled by the rope of the sea anchor.

With her motor throttled well down to give just sufficient steerage way and no more, the *Venture* slowly closed the disabled yacht.

The man in the stern-sheets was standing and holding on to the cockpit-coaming with one hand. The other was tucked into the flap of his oilskin coat.

"Can you take me in tow?" he shouted down wind.

"Aye, aye!" replied Ron. "Stand by to heave us a line."

"Can't!" was the laconic rejoinder. "Wrist crocked!"

"That settles it!" declared the Patrol-leader, addressing the Second. "We'll have to put someone aboard her. I'd go, but——"

"Yes, I know," added Ned. "You're in charge here. I'd better have a shot at it!"

Quickly they discussed and settled the details.

The *Venture* must be manœuvred close enough to the disabled yacht without actually touching, yet near enough for Ned to leap from one craft to the other. As soon as he was on board, Lofty would heave a stout rope to the yacht's fore-deck, which Ned would secure before going aft to take the tiller, in case the owner was incapable of steering.

Already the Sea Scouts had placed fenders in position—not those puny, canvas-covered ones that many yachstmen have mostly for display, but good hefty ones made up out of old rope.

" Easy ahead!" ordered Ron.

He had decided to run alongside to lee'ard, since the yacht's deeper draught would keep her from sagging to a greater extent than the relatively shallow-draughted *Venture*.

Meanwhile Lofty had coiled a fairly heavy grass warp in the stern-sheets, while Ned, having discarded his oilskins for greater freedom of action, stood by the *Venture's* shrouds ready to take his daring leap.

He knew that it was a risky performance. His feet might slip on the yacht's deck with the chance of receiving a stunning blow against the mast; or he might jump short and find himself struggling in the rough sea and in danger of being crushed between the two plunging and rolling craft.

Slowly the *Venture* closed.

" Keep on with that pump!" ordered the Patrol-leader.

A moment or so later Ned jumped.

He landed with his feet on the yacht's coaming. His hands clutched the shrouds. There he hung as the sloop listed outwards;

then, as she recovered, he swung himself inside the shrouds and threw himself flat on the plunging fore-deck.

It was only by gripping the bitts with one hand that he could save himself from being jerked overboard, so lively was the motion of the yacht as she strained at her sea-anchor.

The *Venture* continued to forge ahead. Now her transom was abreast the yacht's stem head.

" Stand by!" shouted Lofty, and made a magnificent cast with the rope.

Deftly Ned took a couple of round turns round the bitts and a fisherman's bend round the mast. He didn't mean to make a mess of things by trusting solely to the bitts when the hawser took up the strain.

" All fast!" he bawled.

Under slightly increased throttle the *Venture* drew ahead.

Ron was now as cool as the proverbial cucumber. He knew exactly what ought to be done and the difficulties involved in taking a craft in tow in a heavy seaway. What was more, he was sure that Lofty knew his job, which was to pay out the tow-rope slowly and to take up the strain gradually.

The Patrol-leader's chief concern was to avoid getting the propeller foul of the rope of the sea-anchor.

Already Ned was heaving this cumbersome

contraption on board by means of the trip-line. Even then it offered so stout a resistance that he was tempted to cut it adrift with his sheath-knife.

"If that merchant has a crippled wrist, how did he manage to get the sea-anchor overboard?" he asked himself, as, with his feet planted firmly against the bitts, he heaved and sweated at the stubborn canvas sea-anchor.

He got it on board at last, though by this time the yacht had gathered considerable way. Drenched to the skin with rain and spray, Ned fought his way aft to the comparative shelter of a small, open cockpit.

"Can you manage, sir?" he asked.

The owner nodded.

"It's a one-handed job and she steers easily," he replied. "Where are you bound?"

"Otherport, sir."

"So was I when this confounded halliard parted. That's when the shackle at the head of the mainsail kippered my wrist. Do you mind hauling those down. They won't be wanted now!"

He indicated the distress signal, the halliard of which was cleated to a fife-rail on the starboard shrouds.

Ned scrambled along the waterway and, with one arm round the shrouds, succeeded in lowering and untoggling the two flags. As he did so it again struck him as rather strange that the yachtsman, after having been partly disabled, had succeeded not only in getting the cumbersome sea-anchor overboard but in running the distress signal up. Even with his two sound arms Ned had his work cut out on the deck of the wildly plunging yacht.

He came aft again. The yachtsman and presumed owner of the *Nut*—for such the name on the brass rudder-head proclaimed her to be—was a tall, lean man of about forty, clean-shaven, and with dark hair turning grey over the temples.

"You're fairly soaked, my lad!" he observed.

"It's nothing, sir," protested Ned. "Salt spray doesn't harm a fellow."

"But rain does, especially when you're out in a chilly wind. You'll find a spare oilskin in the cabin."

It was a command more than a suggestion. Ned went down a couple of steps into the saloon.

What a contrast to the rough-and-ready conditions on board the *Venture*! The roof glistened with white enamel; the bulkheads were of polished teak; on the settee were scarlet cushions. Overhead were electric lamps cunningly recessed into the coach roof. For'ard of the saloon was a sleeping-cabin, but as the doors were closed Ned couldn't see what this place was like.

He found an almost new oilskin hanging in a cupboard and, scrambling into it—no easy task on account of the yacht's violent motions—he returned to the cockpit.

The boom, together with the loosely stowed mainsail, had been hurriedly lashed down, making a decidedly unprofessional job of the stow. In fact the boom-end was awkwardly in the helmsman's way; and although with this sea running it might not remain in the crutch, it could be raised by the topping-lift.

"Shall I top up the boom and stow the mainsail, sir?" asked Ned, anxious that the yacht should present a fairly trim appearance when she made Otherport harbour.

"No!" replied the owner harshly; then, noting the surprised look on the Sea Scout's face, he added in extenuation: "If that boom takes charge you'd be knocked overboard; and there'd be precious little chance of picking you up in this sea!"

Meanwhile the *Venture* was plugging steadily on, with the *Nut* in tow.

Satisfied that the hawser was equal to the job, and that the two Sea Scouts told off to keep the leak under control were " sticking to it ", the Patrol-leader devoted his attention to what lay ahead.

He wasn't at all certain of his position. According to his calculations, the West Rat's Tail buoy should have been sighted on the port bow by this time. Quite possibly, when the operation of taking the yacht in tow was in progress, the set of the tide had swept the *Venture* to the south'ard and in consequence the buoy was lost to sight in the murky atmosphere.

" How about getting those fenders in, Cap'n?" asked Lofty.

" Let them stop," replied Ron.

Placing them in position before running alongside the disabled yacht was an urgent and necessary business, though attended by a certain amount of risk. Although it wasn't " the thing " for a craft to be under way with fenders hanging over her sides, the Patrol-leader had decided to let them remain rather than invite the chance of having some of his crew swept overboard.

"It's clearing a bit," observed Lofty.

"Yes; but where's the buoy?" asked Ron.

Shading his eyes, Lofty scanned the expanse of white-capped waves. Visibility had now increased to about a mile; but neither on the bows nor abeam was there any sign of the much-desired buoy.

"What's that: a boat?" suddenly inquired Wee Jock, who, straightening his back after a spell at the pump, was pointing astern.

"Boat: where?" asked Ron, snatching up the binoculars. "Why, it's the buoy. We've overshot it!"

He didn't add that in consequence the *Venture* and her tow were perilously near the submerged ledge known as the Whelps.

The helm was put down and steadied when the *Venture* had altered course eight points to port. In a few minutes the first of the Other-port fairway buoys was sighted.

The alteration of course had brought the wind abaft the beam, owing also to the fact that it had veered a couple of points.

Although the sea was still running high, Ron felt that a load of responsibility had been lifted from his mind. Happen what might—even a breakdown of the motor—there was a sound chance of winning through. It would be possible to make sail with the now favourable wind.

On the other hand, the difficulties of the tow increased. With the wind abaft the beam the sea threatened to break into the open cockpit, while the *Nut*, owing to the windage of her lofty Bermudan mast, was sagging considerably to lee'ard and rolling heavily.

Another burst of rain blotted out the sky; then, when it cleared, a craft under power could be seen approaching the homeward-bound *Venture*.

"Golly! It's the lifeboat!" exclaimed Musty. "What's she doing? Putting out to look for us?"

"Perhaps our fellows at Old Nick's Hat thought we were in danger, and telephoned for the lifeboat," suggested Hughes.

"Starboard a bit!" ordered the Patrol-leader. "Keep your proper side of the fairway."

The lifeboat, her blue hull with the distinctive red band glistening as she lifted over the waves, was approaching rapidly under power. Her crew, wearing brown canvas-covered lifebelts and red stocking caps, sat motionless as statues except for the coxswain.

Without slowing down—so evidently she wasn't looking for the *Venture*—the lifeboat held on her course. As she passed, the coxswain raised a megaphone.

" 'Tes no place for you lads!" he shouted. " Be thankful you be nigh home!"

" What's wrong, Mr. Bullock?" asked Ron, who, like the rest of the Otherport Sea Scouts, knew every man of the lifeboat's crew.

" Schooner's ashore on——"

The rest of the sentence was tossed to the winds as the lifeboat, partly hidden in clouds of spray, hurried on her errand of mercy.

" It might have been us," declared Lofty soberly.

" Did you think that out there?" asked the Patrol-leader.

" Aye; I wondered if we'd get through," replied the Sea Scout. " Didn't like to put the wind up the others."

The harbour piers were now in sight. Beyond were the grey houses and the red roofs of the town, now bathed in a gleam of sunshine.

The Sea Scouts were considerably elated. They had won through. Not only had they kept the leak under control, but they had rescued the yacht, if not from total loss, from serious mishap.

Twenty minutes later Ron gave the order for the motors to be eased down in order to shorten the towing hawser—a necessary precaution when entering a crowded harbour.

The piers were crowded. Townsfolk who had gone out to give the lifeboat a rousing send-off had waited to welcome the home-coming *Venture*, and to wonder how and why she was towing a yacht nearly twice her size.

As soon as the tow-rope was adjusted to the required length, Ron gave the order for the motor to be run all out. It was pure "swank" on his part, in order to create the impression of smartness amongst the onlookers, who included parents, relations and friends of each member of the Seagull patrol.

The Patrol-leader had not remembered the warning: "Let him that thinketh he standeth take heed lest he fall!"

There was a confused sea running at the entrance to the harbour, set up by the back-wash from the stone piers.

Even as the *Venture* shot between the pier-heads and as Ron raised his arm in acknowledgment of the welcoming cheers from the spectators, a terrific jar shook the little craft from stem to stern.

There was a simultaneous shout of astonishment and consternation from the crew; and as the Patrol-leader gave a quick glance over his shoulder he saw the greater part of the *Venture's* transom, the head of the rudder and the two bollards to which the towing hawser was made fast had been torn away, and were bobbing on the surface in the motor craft's wake.

Water was pouring in through the jagged

gap between the extremities of the two quarters. Unless something could be done to check the inrush or beach the *Venture* within a minute or so, she would sink like a stone.

With the idea of steering for the hard at the inner end of the harbour, Ron put the wheel over to starboard. It turned without resistance. The steering chains were no longer attached to the yoke of the rudder.

"Get an oar out as fast as you can!" ordered the Patrol-leader.

While Lofty was placing the sweep in position to act as a temporary steering oar, the rest of the crew tore off their oilskins and used them in an attempt to stop the inrush of water.

Slowly the *Venture's* bows swung to starboard. She was now well inside the pierhead and in comparatively calm water, and was still carrying a good amount of way. Already the water was above the engine beds. It seemed a toss-up what would happen first: the engine stop or the boat sink.

The Sea Scouts were comparatively calm. There was certainly no sign of panic. On the other hand, there was considerable excitement on the part of the crowds on the piers. People were shouting advice; some of a more practical turn of mind ran to the slip, where several rowing boats were lying, in order to put off to the rescue.

Another hundred yards and the *Venture*

could beach herself. But could she stay the course?

Lower and lower sank her stern, and as it did so the inrush of water correspondingly increased. With a series of poppings in the carburettor the motor petered out.

Still carrying way, though with rapidly diminishing speed, the *Venture* lurched shorewards; but it was now evident that she would not reach there before she foundered.

"Come out of that, Christie!" ordered Ron.

Tom Moore was only just in time. He had stuck to his post, knee deep in water, at the motor. Even as he gained the cockpit the *Venture's* stern dipped. Cascades of water poured over the coamings, and amid a smother of foam and vapour she slid to the bottom of Otherport Harbour, leaving her crew in what is termed in seafaring circles, "the ditch!"

The Sea Scouts were in no danger. Every one of them could swim well; the water was surprisingly warm. But for the fact that they had lost their highly prized *Venture* they would have treated the incident as a joke.

Some of the swimmers were spluttering, having swallowed a mouthful of salt water. Fortunately they had discarded their oilskins, and those who had been wearing seaboots—a practice that ought never to be followed afloat—were able to kick them off.

So far no one had attempted to strike out for the hard. They were just swimming round or treading water, and trying to salvage various articles that had come to the surface from the sunken craft.

Amongst these was a Primus stove floating bottom upwards and looking like a miniature mine; while close to it were two rubber boots with only the toes showing above water owing to a small quantity of air being trapped in them. Oilskins, partly waterlogged, oars, a grating, a water-beaker and a couple of petrol tins comprised some of the " souvenirs " the swimmers had rescued from the wreck.

Meanwhile the *Nut*, left to her own devices, had also gained shelter. She had carried sufficient way to shoot the pierheads and had drifted alongside a staging to which she had made fast; so Ron and his chums hadn't to worry about her or their chum who was on board.

By this time boats were upon the scene and the swimmers were taken on board. They were now more aware of the serious nature of the accident. They had lost the *Venture*. More so than his chums, the Patrol-leader was feeling a bit down in the mouth, wondering whether it was due to any fault of his—perhaps he oughtn't to have given the order for full speed ahead—that the motor cruiser's stern had been torn clean out of her.

" A rum go, I'll allow," declared an ancient salt in the boat that had picked Ron up. " I could hardly believe my eyes when that there transom flew right up in the air!"

" Now if it 'ud 'appened out there!" added another, a fisherman, jerking his thumb in a direction seawards, " I shouldn't 'a wondered. Nasty lumps o' sea. And wot's that craft you gived a pluck to?"

" She's the *Nut*, I believe," replied Ron.

" Nutshell 'ud be more the mark!" rejoined the first man. " Stranger to these parts;

leastways I've never set eyes on 'er afore! Reckon you can sting her owners for a tidy drop o' salvage."

Salvage! Ron hadn't considered that possibility. It might go towards the repairs to the *Venture*, if she were worth repairing.

And yet, somehow, the Patrol-leader didn't like the idea. For one thing, the Sea Scouts were merely doing their Good Turn without asking for a reward; for another, it seemed unfair to take advantage of another's misfortunes. It wasn't keeping up the traditions of the Brotherhood of the Sea.

"I wouldn't think twice about it," declared the old fisherman. "The owner'll be insured. Even if he isn't, if he owns a yot he can afford to pay. It's up to you, lad! You've put your craft under while givin' yon yot a pluck-in. Did she ask for it?"

"She was flying a distress signal."

"Then that settles it! You've a clear case for salvage. I reckon the tide'll leave the *Venture* high and dry come six this afternoon and then you chaps can see if she's worth repairin'."

The boat ran alongside the slipway and landed the saturated crew of the lost *Venture*. Here they separated, going to their respective homes for a change of clothing, having arranged to meet at five o'clock to see what could be done to refloat the wreck.

Ron Bradley had a lot to do before then.

He would have to look up his Scoutmaster—it happened to be visiting day at the hospital—and break the news that the *Venture* had met with misfortune, perhaps disaster.

Before doing that he decided to obtain Ned Henderson's version of the mishap and to hear how the *Nut* had fared after she found herself adrift.

It seemed rather strange, he thought, that Ned hadn't looked him up on his way home, because the Second hadn't had a ducking, and therefore had not to shift into dry clothes.

So, having had a belated meal, Ron went round to his chum's house.

"Ned? He isn't home yet," replied Mrs. Henderson. "I thought he was with you."

Evidently the Second's parent had not heard of the mishap, which was not to be wondered at, since infirmity had kept her in the house except on very fine days.

Briefly Ron explained the situation, reassuring her that Ned must be all right, since he had seen the yacht, with the Sea Scout on board, safely moored in the harbour.

"I'll run down and see what he's doing, Mrs. Henderson," he added. "Shall I send him along?"

"Yes, do; the poor boy must be simply starving."

The *Nut* had not been shifted from the berth in which she had been placed. To get to her, Ron had to descend a vertical ladder set in the stone wall of the quay and thence to a floating pontoon against which the yacht lay.

By this time she presented a more ship-shape appearance. Although a new main halliard had not been rove, the mainsail had been properly stowed and the boom had been placed in the boom-crutch. The cabin doors were open, but there were no signs either of Ned or the owner.

"*Nut* ahoy!" hailed the Patrol-leader.

It was Ned who answered.

The Second was smiling delightedly. Apparently the loss of the Venture had not damped his spirits. There were also obvious signs that he had been interrupted in the midst of a hearty meal.

"Good news, Ron!" he exclaimed. "Mr. Gunville—that's the owner—is going to—— But I'd better start at the beginning! Come aboard: I'm in charge until he returns."

"Let's hear your good news, Ned," said the Patrol-leader, as he followed his chum into the cabin, where the best part of a veal and ham pie showed that the Second was certainly doing himself well. "Fire away!"

"At first I wasn't sure of Mr. Gunville," began Ned. "When I offered to stow some of the gear, he ticked me off, though he added he was afraid I'd be pitched overboard. You bet I'd take jolly good care I wasn't! Well, just as we were entering the harbour I saw the *Venture's* transom torn clean away. It was a comic sight to see the look of astonishment on you fellows' faces! Of course, I didn't know then that she was going to sink; in any case, I had my work cut out."

" What did you do?"

" The *Nut* was carrying a fair amount of way, but I didn't think she'd shoot between the pier-heads unless something was done about it. So I nipped up for'ard, set the staysail and then sheeted it home. The wind was just enough abaft the beam for the staysail to get us in."

" Did the owner—what did you say his name is?"

" Gunville—Mr. Tarrant Gunville."

" Did he order you to hoist the sail?"

" No: and I didn't wait to be told. I just did it on my own. He seemed rather pleased about it, although I didn't think he would be, and when we'd run alongside he asked me if I'd mind hanging on while he went to see a doctor about his wrist, and also he wanted to telephone to someone in London. I said I didn't mind in the least, as I saw you fellows had been picked up by old Sampson. While he was changing into shore-going things—and it took some time, with his damaged arm—he asked a lot of questions about the

Troop and particularly our patrol. Then he said he wasn't responsible for the smash——"

"He wasn't," agreed Ron.

"And that there couldn't be a case of salvage."

The Patrol-leader bridled at that. Although he was against the payment of salvage money on principle, it struck him as being rather petty that Tarrant Gunville should try to evade his liability.

"Why not?" he asked. "He'd hoisted the N.C.—the distress signal."

"Yes, but the *Venture* failed to tow the *Nut* into a place of safety. The *Nut* made it under her own canvas and so the implied contract wasn't carried out in its entirety. Those were his words."

"He seems a bit of a slippery customer," observed Ron. "And what's this he says he's going to do?"

"I'm coming to that. Well, you see, he asked a lot more questions, then he told me he wasn't going to split hairs over a salvage question and that, as he admired the way we came alongside and took the *Nut* in tow, he'd buy us a motor cruiser to take her place: not a new one, but a jolly sound second-hand one that's for sale at Easthaven."

"That's jolly decent of him!" exclaimed the Patrol-leader. "Easthaven: that's seventy or eighty miles from here."

"That's where the *Nut* is usually kept," explained Ned. "He's coming up to the Den at eight o'clock this evening to tell the fellows all about his offer."

Ron considered the matter. The wreck of the *Venture* would be left high and dry by six o'clock. There might be time to bale her out and fix up a temporary covering of painted canvas over the gaping transom by seven. The patrol could then shift into uniform and be at the Den by eight o'clock, ready to receive the generous Mr. Gunville. By ten o'clock the *Venture* would have been refloated by the rising tide. It would be probably midnight before the job of hauling her out above high-water mark could be completed; but the Sea Scouts were used to working by tide rather than by time.

"All right, I'll fix it up with the other fellows," he decided. "I wish the Skipper could be there; I'm seeing him this afternoon and the news will buck him up no end. I don't mind telling him of what happened to the old *Venture* now. Well, is that all Mr. Gunville said?"

"Mostly," replied Ned, grinning; "except that he told me to get busy on the pie. Have some? It's jolly good!"

Before Ron could reply the yacht heeled under the weight of a heavy person stepping on the waterways. The intruder stepped down upon the cockpit gratings and, bending, peered into the cabin.

He wore the uniform of the Customs Service.

The Otherport Sea Scouts knew most of the Customs Waterguard in the district either personally or by sight—mainly the former—but this was a stranger.

"Good afternoon!" he greeted them. "Owner aboard?"

"No, he's ashore," replied Ned.

"H'm!" ejaculated the officer in a disappointed tone. Then, as his eyes grew accustomed to the comparative gloom of the cabin, he caught sight of the name on the Second's jersey. "You belong here, then. And this other young gentleman?"

"He's a Sea Scout too; only he's not in uniform," replied Ned. "He had a ducking when the *Venture* sank."

"So you were one of them," rejoined the man, his grim features relaxing in a smile. "I heard about it, but I wasn't on duty at the time. My name's Badger, if that's of any interest to you, and I've only just been transferred from Crowhaven to Otherport. But I didn't pay you a visit just to introduce myself, although I'm always pleased to make the acquaintance of Sea Scouts—my young brother happens to be one. What I've come aboard for is to take down a few particulars. The name of this craft is the *Nut*, I understand?"

"Yes, Mr. Badger."

Mr. Badger glanced at the smooth, white enamelled main beam. There were no figures cut deeply into it, as would have been the case had the yacht been entered in the records of the Board of Trade.

"H'm; no registered number. Is she in Lloyds?"

"I can't say," replied Ned.

"Neither can I until I get back to the office," observed the Customs officer. "Does she belong to a 'recognized' yacht club? She's not flying a burgee, I notice."

Again Ned had to express his ignorance.

"Well, where's she from? Is she come foreign?"

"From Easthaven, I believe. You see, I've been left in charge till Mr. Gunville—that's the owner—returns."

"Ah, well!" rejoined Mr. Badger. "In that case I'll have a look round. If you don't mind sitting here. You'll be out of my way and you can see how a Customs man has to work hard for his living!"

From the side pocket of his uniform monkey-jacket he produced a serviceable-looking screwdriver and a thin steel graduated rod. Then he removed his jacket and laid it on the settee and started operations.

Up came the floorboards, revealing a ton or so of rusty iron ballast. With the steel rod he prodded between the pigs of ballast; but, judging by the disappointed expression on his face, his efforts did not produce the anticipated result.

Then he tried the space between the panels and the yacht's side, removing the cushions for the purpose. Every nook and cranny in the saloon was systematically explored in a way that astonished the boys by its thoroughness in a vain search for contraband.

"Well, we'll try our luck in there next," announced Mr. Badger, with renewed cheerfulness, as he pointed to the door of the fore-cabin.

Most of the diminutive space was occupied by a folded canvas dinghy. This the Customs man partly extended as a possible hiding-place for dutiable articles. Again drawing blank, he removed the blankets and cushions from the bunk, explored the lockers underneath, tapped the deck beams to assure himself that they were not hollow and designed hiding-places for smuggled drugs, and measured the thickness of the bulkheads to see that they were not doubled.

All this the two Sea Scouts watched with

great interest, although they wondered who was going to set the cabin right again: Mr. Badger, themselves, or the still absent Mr. Gunville. And what would he have to say on his return?

Admitting defeat below, the Customs man went on deck, followed by Ron and Ned. By this time quite a crowd of interested onlookers had gathered on the quay. There always seem plenty of people to watch others at work!

Mr. Badger tapped the mast, which, like a good many on Bermuda-rigged yachts, was hollow. It looked as if he were about to prod a hole in it with his rod, then he barked out a question:

"When was the sail stowed?"

"Just before noon," replied Ned. "I did it."

"Nothing wrapped up in it?" though it sounded an absurd question.

"No, I'm certain of that."

"Right! Now I'll have a look in this locker."

He went on his hands and knees and inserted the upper half of his bulk into the sail-locker under the short counter. As a natural result he had deprived himself of daylight, and, not having a torch in his possession, had to grope. In so doing he bumped his skull against the rudder trunk and barked his knuckles on an exposed bolt-head, but seemed to take such mishaps as a matter of course.

Mr. Badger was still in this ostrich-like undignified posture when Tarrant Gunville, his bandaged arm supported by a sling, stepped on board.

All he saw were the bulging nether garments of the Customs man; there was nothing visible to show his official status and his attitude seemed curious for a visitor.

" What's this?" demanded Mr. Gunville heatedly. " Who's this fellow? I left you in charge, and this is what I find: a beachcomber rummaging in my yacht and you standing by and doing nothing!"

" It's a Customs officer, sir!" declared Ned.

" Oh!"

The angry expression on the owner's face gave place to a conciliatory smile as Mr. Badger emerged, puffing and blowing with his exertions in the confined space.

" Good afternoon, sir!" began the Customs man. " Just having a rummage round in the execution of my duty!"

" So it would seem from the first view I got," rejoined Mr. Gunville. " And what have you found?"

" A nasty bit of copper bolt," replied Mr. Badger, as he sucked his gory knuckles. " Otherwise nothing—yet."

" And you won't," added the yachtsman cheerfully; then, peering into the cabin and seeing its disordered state, he blazed up again: "This is outrageous, turning my things inside out while I'm away!"

"There's no need to lose your patience, sir, and of course I regret——"

"No need to lose my patience? Isn't there? I'll have to see about this. You've grossly exceeded your duties."

"Oh no, sir! This yacht comes in here—in distress, so I'm told—and you go ashore without giving us any particulars or declaring you aren't come 'foreign'. The yacht isn't registered; she doesn't belong to a recognized club, and if that isn't a bit fishy, what is? These young gentlemen here couldn't give me the particulars I wanted; so, in the absence of a declaration to the contrary, I concluded the yacht has come across Channel from a French port."

"Wrong again!" exclaimed Mr. Gunville. "She's from her home port, Easthaven. I put into Dockingham yesterday, where the Customs asked my last port and intended destination. I never was beyond ten miles of the English coast all the trip."

"Well, you'd have saved both of us a lot of trouble if you'd given *us* particulars, sir," declared Mr. Badger, as he put on his monkey-jacket. "How about this lash-up? Shall I bear a hand to set things straight before I say good afternoon?"

" No, thanks! I'll see to that," replied Mr. Gunville. " Good afternoon!"

Mr. Badger made a ponderous exit and, climbing the ladder, made his way through the crowd of distinctly disapproving onlookers, many of whom had been expecting to see him staggering under the burden of a couple of filled rum-jars!

" Shall we tidy up, sir?" asked the Patrol-leader.

" It will be very sporting if you do, though I'm sorry to trouble you—my arm, you know. Nothing serious, and it will be all right again in a day or so."

CHAPTER VI THE ABSENT GUEST OF HONOUR

Just before six the Seagulls, wearing their oldest clothes and rubber knee-boots, assembled at the harbour to carry out salvage operations on the *Venture*.

Very disreputable she looked as the falling tide exposed her to view. She was lying with a slight list to starboard. Already seaweed and the usual garbage of a tidal harbour were covering her deck, while her paintwork was discoloured by stains from the oil that had escaped from the submerged motor. The fore-hatch cover had floated away, as had the engine cover and part of the casing. Over the cabin floor there was water trapped to a depth of about a couple of feet, and on it floated locker covers, sodden cushions and a miscellaneous collection of flotsam from the cabin and galley.

There were, as usual, plenty of idle onlookers. Tom Briskett, the man who had sold the *Venture* to the Troop, wasn't among them. He had been, but he discreetly cleared off before the Seagulls arrived upon the scene—and for a very good reason!

In spite of his assurances to the contrary, the *Venture* was as rotten as a bad pear. The teak sides were in sound condition, but the transom, that for some reason was of elm, had been eaten through and through by that insidious disease known as dry rot. Outwardly there were no signs of it. Paint, like charity, covers a multitude of sins, and in this case it was hard-gloss enamel that had successfully hidden the decayed wood until it gave way under the strain of a towed yacht.

" We may be able to fit a new stern and sell her for what she'll fetch," suggested Ron hopefully. " I wonder what the motor's like?"

" It won't be much the worse after I've overhauled it," declared Christie Moore confidently. " Pity I hadn't time to slip off the magneto before she filled. It may want rewinding, but I'll try baking it in an oven first."

" Don't waste time, lads!" exclaimed the Patrol-leader. " Tide'll be making soon. Start baling her out while Ned and I patch up the stern."

All hands set to work with a will, using buckets, saucepans and frying-pans to throw out the accumulated water.

While this task was in progress, Ron and Ned tacked on a piece of tarred canvas across the gap where the transom had been. Over the edges of the canvas stout battens were secured by screws in order to make the job reasonably watertight.

Christie and Musty, those energetic and indefatigable amateur engineers, were already on board, " slipping " the magneto, draining the crank-case and pouring paraffin through the sparking-plug apertures in order to guard against the motor " rusting up " through immersion in salt water. Then the carburettor had to receive attention. Knowing that every hour meant increased damage to the engine, the two youths worked against time, without waiting for the salvaged *Venture* to be hauled up at " Bungs " Cotter's yard.

It is a remarkable fact that wherever Sea Scout troops are formed these attract plenty of friends, especially amongst the seafaring population. Men of means, men of leisure and men in humble circumstances readily do their good turns to the lads even as the Scouts' perform theirs to others.

Amongst the Otherport Troop's friends was Mr. " Bungs " Cotter, who earned a modest livelihood as a boat-builder and repairer. At one time in his career he had been a leading shipwright in the Royal Navy.

" Put the *Venture* ashore in my yard, lads !" was his spontaneous invitation. " There's a mort o' room and she can stop there until you make up your minds what to do wi' her. How much do I charge? A penny a foot overall length to most folk; to you—nothing! 'Cos why? 'Cos you're a likely crowd of lads and not like those larrikins knocking around and always up to mischief. More'n once you've given me a hand and now it's up to me to do summat for you. She should be afloat about eleven. I'll lend you a dinghy to tow her across and I'll have the heaving-up gear ready. We should have her up by midnight."

At 7.15 p.m. the preliminary repairs were completed, and seven bedraggled, mud-plastered youths, with their hands covered with tar, floundered through the slime left by the tide and climbed the ladder to the top of the quay.

At five minutes to eight the same fellows, with clean, shining faces and spotless hands—paraffin and then soap and *cold* water had removed all traces of tar—and in their smart and serviceable uniforms were waiting at the Otherport Sea Scouts' "guard-ship", which wasn't a ship in the truest sense of the word but a spacious loft over a disused rope-walk.

The loft had been converted to resemble as much as possible the main-deck of an old-time sailing-ship. The small windows that in day-time commanded a view across the harbour to the open sea looked very much like gun-ports. The ladder from the ground was an old ship's one, with brass treads, brightly polished, and white cotton man-ropes. The floor was of oak, and had been scrubbed and washed so frequently that it would have earned praise from the most exacting Commander in the Royal Navy.

Long deal tables, for the occasion unshipped and stowed against a " bulkhead ", wooden forms, and even hammocks slung from beams at one end of the " deck ", added to the nautical atmosphere.

At the other end of the den the bulkhead had been draped with signal flags. One string of coloured bunting spelt the word WELCOME, and was supported by suitable devices composed of oars, boathooks, lifebuoys, lifebelts and hand-signalling flags.

These preparations had not been carried out by the Seagulls. They had been very busy in another direction. The news of Tarrant Gunville's impending visit had spread. So had the object of it—the formal presentation of a motor cruiser to the Troop.

The Otters, Seamews and Seals had been responsible for the cheerful atmosphere of the den, and they had rolled up in full strength. So had about twenty adults, some of them the fathers of Sea Scouts, others who had the cause at heart, and a few had " gate-crashed ", mainly through motives of curiosity.

Amongst them was Mr. Badger, who was

now off duty, and who had given one of his subordinates instructions to keep an eye on the *Nut* during her owner's visit to the Sea Scouts' guard-ship, just in case any evil-disposed person should attempt to pilfer from the yacht.

There was one absentee who would be greatly missed: Scoutmaster Dyson, now in hospital. Although absent in body he would be present in mind, was the firm conviction of every Sea Scout in the den.

However, there was Group Scoutmaster Miles, a keen, efficient, elderly man of whom most of the Sea Scouts stood in awe. He was not of them, like Mr. Dyson, but, in spite of his efforts to the contrary, a being on a higher plane.

The four patrol-leaders stood at the head of the companion ladder ready to escort the guest of the evening to a chair on the "quarter-deck".

Eight bells were struck; the Sea Scouts detailed to pipe the visitor aboard raised their whistles to their lips, waited and then lowered them again.

Ron hurried down the ladder and into the road. Except for a few fishermen there was no one in sight.

"Can't see him anywhere," he announced to his fellow patrol-leaders.

"He knew where to find us?"

" Rather! He asked and I told him."

" Gosh! Is it going to be a leg-pull?" asked the P.L. of the Seals. " What if he's set sail on the flood tide now the wind's dropped?"

" The *Nut* was alongside the stage when we left at a quarter past seven. Hadn't we better start with a few sea shanties to keep the fellows busy till Mr. Gunville arrives?"

" May as well," agreed the Seagull's patrol-leader. " All the same, Ron, you'd better get ready to make a speech regretting Mr. Tarrant Gunville's absence!"

The dread that, after all, Mr. Gunville had played a rather senseless practical joke upon the Sea Scouts began to grip Ron's mind. He found himself wishing that he hadn't made such a splash over the evening's business and had kept his mouth shut about the magnificent gift of a motor cruiser!

The four patrol-leaders returned to the den. As soon as their heads appeared above the coaming of the companion-way, the place rang with the shrill trills of the bo'sun's pipes and the loud cheers of the enthusiastic Sea Scouts.

Ron held up his hand for silence.

" Sorry, you chaps! Mr. Gunville hasn't arrived yet. We'll get busy with ' Rolling down to Rio '."

The boys sang with a will and the rollicking tune was taken up by their elders.

Ron went across to Mr. Miles.

" What ought we to do about it, sir?" he asked in a low voice. " It looks as if we've been let down."

" You're sure Mr. Gunville arranged for eight o'clock?" asked the Group Scoutmaster.

" Sure."

" Something may have detained him. We'll carry on till eight-thirty, and then, if he doesn't arrive, I'd better say a few words. I suppose I can accept the gift, even in the donor's absence, on the strength of his promise to you?"

" Not to me, sir. To Ned Henderson."

" You heard him give it?"

" No, sir."

" H'm; well, carry on, Ron! We'll have to make the best of it and keep smiling, even if he doesn't roll up."

Half past eight and no Tarrant Gunville.

The singers, breathless with their exertions, brought " Shenandoah " to a close. There was an uncomfortable silence until the elder members of the party began asking one another questions in a low voice as to why the guest of the evening hadn't arrived.

Meanwhile Ned Henderson had gone down to the harbour.

The *Nut* was still there. There was no light visible through the cabin scuttle. On the quay-side a greatcoated man was walking stolidly to and fro. Ned recognized him as a Customs boatman.

"Have you seen anything of Mr. Gunville, the owner of the yacht?" asked the Second.

"Yes," was the reply. "He went ashore just before eight; say about ten to."

"Did he say where he was going?"

"No; I don't think he saw me."

"In what direction did he go?"

"Towards your guard-ship. Hasn't he shown up?"

"No; we can't think why."

The boatman gave a low whistle.

"Think he's stopped to have a drink with some pals?" he suggested.

"Hardly. He's a stranger here. Well, thanks for the information. I'll get back and let the others know. Did he lock the cabin door before he went?"

"I don't know. He may have done. I didn't see him until he was up the ladder. You can see if you like; I'll give you a light."

The boatman switched on his electric torch. Ned climbed down the ladder, crossed the pontoon and stepped into the *Nut's* cockpit. He tried the double doors. They were locked.

Ned returned to the den just as the Group Scoutmaster was finishing a long and rather unsatisfactory speech.

Mr. Miles had done his best to make the

most of the facts at his disposal. He thanked the absent donor for his really magnificent gift that, although not yet actually presented, was more or less waiting at Easthaven. No doubt there were sound reasons why Mr. Gunville was unable to be present that evening, notwithstanding his avowed decision to do so, and in his regrettable absence there was but one thing that the Sea Scouts could do, and that was to pass a hearty vote of thanks for the gift that had been promised. He looked forward to the time when the——

The Group Scoutmaster paused. It had just occurred to him that he did not know the name of the promised motor cruiser.

"Do you know her name, Ron?" he whispered.

"No, sir!"

The Patrol-leader passed the question on to his Second.

"I don't know," replied Ned.

"And so," concluded Mr. Miles, "we can look forward with pleasure and gratitude to the time when this unnamed—I mean the craft whose name is as yet unknown to us—will be lying on her moorings in Otherport Harbour as a constant reminder of our generous friend, Mr. Tarrant Gunville!"

The Sea Scouts cheered. They weren't at all certain what it all meant. Then an ancient mariner from the back benches observed, loud enough for most of the audience to hear:

" It ain't no deal till the papers are 'anded over!"

Mr. Badger smiled sardonically.

" Those are my sentiments!" he added.

CHAPTER VII — A MIDNIGHT MYSTERY

At ten o'clock the meeting broke up. In a way it had been a disappointment, although the Sea Scouts had let themselves go with their vocal efforts.

The Seagulls hurried off to shift into working rig, for another two hours' work lay in front of them before the *Venture* was hauled out.

At a quarter past the hour Ron made his way towards the harbour. It was now a clear starlight night with hardly a breath of wind. The tide was at its full, and the calm surface of the water reflected the scintillating lights of the pier-heads and the star-powdered sky overhead.

He had just reached the steps alongside of which Mr. "Bungs" Cotter's dinghy was made fast when he noticed two of the Customs men approaching. As they drew nearer he recognized one as Mr. Badger and the other the boatman who had been left to keep an eye on the *Nut*.

"He's not back yet," announced Mr. Badger, without waiting for Ron to ask the question. "There's no object in keeping a watch on the yacht while you fellows are about. And I rather enjoyed myself at your show! Good night! Your little craft's afloat and she doesn't seem to be taking any in!"

Ron waited a few minutes until he was joined by the rest of the patrol, with the exception of Wee Jock, who, somewhat to his disappointment, had been refused permission by his parents to take further part in the salvage operations that night.

From where he stood the Patrol-leader could see the *Venture* with tolerable distinctness as she rode to her own anchor. Night had hidden her scars and the ignominious smears of tar. She looked as shipshape as of yore and, as the Customs officer had mentioned, as if she hadn't leaked a drop.

On the other side of the harbour the *Nut* was hardly distinguishable against the stone wall of the quay, although her slender mast stood out sharply against the starry sky. Her cabin was in darkness, so it seemed fairly certain that her owner had not returned. Perhaps, thought Rob, Mr. Gunville's sprained wrist had given him increased pain and he had gone to a hotel rather than spend a restless night in his bunk; but then, surely he would have sent someone with a message to the guard-ship explaining the reason for his failure to carry out his promise to attend?

As soon as the party was complete the Sea

Scouts boarded the dinghy—a fairly tubby craft—and pulled out to the *Venture*.

Their temporary repairs had been effective. The little craft, although her timbers and interior planking reeked with moisture, was perfectly tight.

Manned by the two inseparables, Musty and Christie, the dinghy went ahead with a warp from her after thwart made fast to the bitts on the *Venture's* fore-deck.

The cruiser's anchor was then hauled aboard and, with Ned steering with a sweep, she gathered way in tow of the dinghy.

There was nothing else moving in the harbour. Alongside the quay the fishing-fleet lay silent and deserted. Moored between two large buoys in the middle of the harbour was a large foreign steamer, her well-decks piled high with Swedish deals. She, too, was in darkness, except for her riding-light.

"It's a wonder some of that deck cargo wasn't washed overboard," observed Ned. "When did she arrive, I wonder?"

"After we'd finished patching up our craft," declared Ron. "The Customs haven't wasted time if they've cleared her already. Hello! There's Mr. Cotter with a lantern. Easy strokes there, you fellows. Way 'nough!"

Lofty nipped for'ard to cast off the tow-line, lest the heavier *Venture* should overrun the dinghy.

"Starboard!" bawled the boatyard owner, waving his lantern. "At that! Helm 'midships!"

There was a slight jar as the *Venture* glided fairly and squarely upon the submerged cradle of the slipway. The crew waded ashore and, under Mr. Cotter's directions, manned the winch.

Slowly but unhesitatingly the *Venture*, looking immense in the starlight, left the water until she was well above the reach of the highest tides.

"That'll do!" declared the boat-builder. "She won't hurt there till to-morrow. Then when you come along we'll strike her over under cover."

"Twelve o'clock!" exclaimed Ned, as the first stroke of midnight echoed across the harbour from the town hall clock. "How the time's gone!"

"Allus does when you're busy," rejoined Mr. Cotter. "Time all of us piped down and turned in. You'd better take the dinghy. It'll save a long walk round by the bridge. Leave her against the steps and I'll send young Bill across for her come mornin'."

Thanking their elderly friend, the Sea Scouts pushed off in the borrowed dinghy. This time Lofty and George took the oars, rowing with long steady strokes so that almost the only sound was the gentle plash of the blades and the ripple of the water against the boat's forefoot.

They passed close to the starboard side of the Swedish steamer. A man's head and shoulders silhouetted against the sky appeared over the rail. He gave a glance at the passing boat and disappeared from sight. Since the dinghy was not running alongside, what she was doing at that time of night was no concern of his. A thin column of steam rose vertically and silently from the steam-pipe abaft the funnel. Everything on board seemed still. The vessel might have been a ghost ship.

As the dinghy drew clear of the steamer's squat counter, Ron leant forward.

"Lay on your oars!" he ordered in a low voice.

Being good seamen and well trained, the two rowers obeyed promptly and without asking the reason why. All the same, they looked over their shoulders in the direction to where the Patrol-leader was pointing.

Fifty or sixty yards or more across the harbour two men were staggering along the east pier under a weighty bundle.

Instinctively Ron realized that there was dirty work on the way. Although it might have been two belated fishermen carrying a bundle of nets down to their boats, he knew that the fishing-fleet did not berth on that side of the harbour. What made the affair suspicious was the fact that the men were going towards the floating stage where the *Nut* lay moored, and were crouching close to the parapet in order to conceal their movements from the watch-house.

"That tall chap," whispered Ned. "Is that Mr. Gunville?"

"No; at least I don't think so," replied Ron. "They're going to dump that gear on board the *Nut*, I think. Together, lads, as quietly as you can. We'll get a closer look at what they're up to."

The rowers had not made more than half a dozen strokes when one of the men caught sight of the silently approaching dinghy.

His companion had descended the ladder to the pontoon, which, owing to the high tide, was now only about five feet below the edge of the quay. He was extending his arms to take the bundle from the other man when the latter suddenly took to his heels.

The bundle dropped with a dull thud to the deck of the float, while the fellow who should have received it swarmed up the ladder and fled in the direction his companion had taken.

This suspicious action was in itself quite sufficient for the Seagulls to raise the alarm.

The harbour echoed to the shrill blast of the Patrol-leader's whistle.

"Give way for all you're worth!" he ordered.

The heavy dinghy leapt forward under the vigorous and powerful strokes of the rowers, as Ron steered towards the floating stage where the *Nut* was lying.

What the trouble was all about the Sea Scouts didn't know. One of the two fugitives might have been Gunville, but what could have been his object in taking to his heels? He had a perfect right, within certain limits, to take gear on board his yacht, even if the time was past midnight. Again, if his wrist had been so severely injured as to necessitate its being put into splints, how could he be carrying part of what certainly was a heavy burden?

A light flashed from the Customs watch-tower. On board the Swedish steamship the Patrol-leader's whistle seemed to have been ignored, even though the dinghy was not more than ten yards off when the alarm was raised. There were no signs of life in the boat-yard where the *Venture* had been hauled out. Evidently Mr. Cotter had lost no time in packing up and going home.

To avoid running alongside the *Nut* and crossing her deck, Ron steered the dinghy to the end of the stage, where there was just enough room to round-to between the wall and the yacht's counter.

The Sea Scouts disembarked; Lofty bent

the painter to a ring-bolt; Ron flashed his torch upon an elongated bundle lying perilously close to the gap that separated the landing-stage from the quay wall.

" It's an old sail rolled up!" declared Musty.

" If it is, why should those chaps run?" asked Ron. " There must be something inside."

At the back of his mind, the Patrol-leader was wondering what the contents of the bundle might be—something in the nature of contraband goods; for although the main thing the Customs bothered themselves with were dutiable imported goods there were such things as war-material that ordinarily could not be sent abroad except under licence, and therefore offered a paying proposition to any unscrupulous persons who would run the risk.

The Sea Scouts never bargained for the actual contents of the mysterious bundle!

" Cut the lashings and see what it is," suggested Lofty.

" No; we'd better not disturb anything till the Customs people arrive," decided Ron.

" They don't appear to be hurrying themselves!" observed Lofty, standing up, so that his head was above the level of the adjoining quay. " The fellows who dumped this here might be a mile away by this time."

In the light of a torch Ned stooped and gingerly prodded the stiff canvas.

"Good heavens!" he ejaculated in an awed voice. "It's a corpse!"

"It may not be!" rejoined the practically minded Patrol-leader, reversing his previous decision. "We'll soon see! Hold my torch, one of you!"

With steady fingers—he was surprised at the calm, deliberate way he went about the unpleasant task—Ron undid the reef knot of the cord. His seaman's instinct prevented him from taking drastic measures by using his sheath-knife.

The edges of the stiff canvas were drawn together and secured by a simple lashing passing through a number of brass eyelets. When half a dozen of these eyelets were unrove, Ron lifted the edges of the canvas aside, revealing the waxen features of a man.

The victim of the fleeing miscreants was Tarrant Gunville!

" Is he dead?" asked Ned.

Before replying, the Patrol-leader placed his hand over Mr. Gunville's heart. As he did so he noticed that although his left wrist was still bandaged it was no longer in splints and supported by a sling. The lower part of his face was stained with blood.

" No," he replied. " He's still alive. He's been sand-bagged, I think. Nip along and fetch the police, Musty! Let the Customs people know on your way. And stand back, you others, to give him air."

Coleman ascended the ladder, and ran off along the quay. He hadn't gone more than fifty yards when he met one of the Customs boatmen leisurely walking towards the landing-stage.

" Hello there, young Musty!" exclaimed the man. " Finished your job?"

" It's not that, Mr. Turnbull," replied the Sea Scout. " Something awful has happened. Didn't you hear our P.L.'s whistle?"

The boatman ignored the question.

" What is it?" he inquired.

"Mr. Gunville——"

"The gent from that little yacht?"

"Yes! He's been attacked."

"Heart attack, you mean?"

"No, by two men. You didn't notice them running off?"

"No, I didn't. All right, I'll get along to see what's up. You'd better inform the police. It's their job!"

"That's where I'm going," rejoined Musty.

Turnbull took a few steps and then stopped to consider. As he had remarked, it wasn't his job to investigate a case of assault. He was there for the examination of vessels arriving "from foreign". All the same, he'd better report to Mr. Badger, which meant waking that worthy up, since it was reasonable to conclude he was sound asleep at home. He rather wondered whether the Customs House Officer would resent being hauled out of bed, since on the face of things there was no question of anyone attempting to land a contraband cargo.

So the boatman went back to the watch-house and, after consulting his colleague, telephoned to the efficient Mr. Badger.

By this time Musty had arrived at the police station, where a burly sergeant, in his shirt-sleeves and smoking a pipe, was whiling away the usually eventless night hours.

"Hello, Musty!" he exclaimed, for the

Otherport Sea Scouts were well known both to the police and the Customs people. "What's wrong? One of your fellows tumbled overboard and drowned?"

"No, Sergeant; Mr. Gunville—he's been found unconscious."

"Gunville—Gunville: who is he?"

"The gentleman in the yacht *Nut.* We towed her in this morning—yesterday morning, I mean."

The sergeant felt in the pocket of his discarded tunic and produced his note-book.

"We'll get this down," he declared. "At 12.30 a.m. on Wednesday the 12th day of August——"

"Look here, Sergeant," interrupted Musty, "hadn't you better send someone at once? Mr. Gunville has been knocked senseless by two men——"

"You witnessed the assault?"

"No, but we—that is the Seagull Patrol—saw them dump him, tied up in canvas, over the quay."

"Into the harbour?"

"No, on the pontoon against the East Pier."

The sergeant stood up and pressed an electric bell. As he was putting on his tunic he asked Musty if he could give a description of the two alleged assailants.

"They were too far off, Sergeant!" replied the Sea Scout.

A constable entered.

"Case of assault on the East Pier, Thompson!" announced the sergeant. "Two of you had better go down with a stretcher. I'll be along presently."

The Law, once set in motion, began to work swiftly.

By telephone the sergeant rang up the Police Surgeon and then warned all constables on point duty to look out for any suspicious characters who might be seen leaving the town. Mobile police both in cars and on motor cycles were ordered to patrol the roads and stop all cars proceeding away from Otherport. The drivers were to be interrogated and, if unable to give a good account of themselves, were to be detained.

"The two men have had a quarter of an hour's start," added the sergeant before replacing the receiver; "so if they've used a car to make their getaway they'll be outside the county by this time. . . . Now, Musty, we'll be getting along."

The main street of Otherport was quiet and deserted as Musty and the sergeant made their way towards the harbour, but as they approached the fishmarket they were joined by Mr. Badger, who, strangely enough, had showed no displeasure at being called up when off duty.

"Mornin', Sergeant! What's all this about?"

" Case of alleged assault and battery, Mr. Badger. A Mr. Gunville: know anthing about him, he being a yachtsman?"

" I've interviewed him," replied the Customs Officer with relish. " I rummaged the yacht yesterday."

" Found anything suspicious?"

" No; but I have hopes!"

Perhaps he was about to elaborate his point when he remembered that the Sea Scout was with them. The rest of the way was covered in silence.

Already there were about twenty persons on the spot, where two lanterns threw a weird light upon the scene. On the quay side was the police stretcher that for the last twenty years had been variously employed in removing " drunks ", injured and dead motorists, corpses recovered from the harbour, and victims of a dozen other cases that brought work for the constabulary and " copy " for the local reporters. It was not, then, surprising to find that, thanks to the co-operation of a friendly policeman, one of the Press representatives, wearing an overcoat over his pyjamas and with his feet encased in carpet slippers, was on the spot and making copious hieroglyphic notes that within a few hours would blossom into a sensational front page column of the *Otherport Reminder*.

" Bad concussion, Sergeant!" announced

one of the constables, who displayed on his tunic the silver Maltese Cross denoting his efficiency in First Aid.

" Case of robbery?"

" No, Sergeant. Here are his purse and pocket-book."

" Right! Get him on the stretcher. Now, you Scouts, you'd better be getting off to bed. All except you, Bradley. You're in charge of this—er—patrol, I understand?"

" Yes, Sergeant," replied Ron.

" Then you'll come back to the station and I'll get a statement from you," continued the sergeant. " There's the ambulance," he added, as the headlamps of the vehicle described a semicircle over the water of the harbour, since the East Pier was impracticable for motor traffic.

Ten minutes later quietude and solitude brooded over Otherport Harbour, and Tarrant Gunville, still unconscious, was lying in a hospital bed.

Incidentally it was in the same hospital in which Scoutmaster Dyson was recovering from his illness.

The surgeon was of the opinion that the victim's condition was grave. A constable waited by the bedside for the patient to recover consciousness, since the Law demands that, the unfortunate man's condition notwithstanding, a statement should be obtained giving a description as far as possible of the assailants.

At nine the next morning the decidedly perplexed Superintendent of Police was in consultation with the sergeant who had gone to the scene of the affair. It appeared that Mr. Gunville had recovered consciousness at seven in the morning, but all he said was that he was coming ashore from the yacht just before eight on the previous evening and had just gained the top of the quay when he heard footsteps behind him. That was all he remembered.

According to Ron Bradley's statement, this did not tally with information already given to the police. Two men had been seen by six of the Seagull Patrol coming towards the landing-stage with a burden afterwards found to be the unconscious Gunville. There could be no sound reason why, if the attack had been made when the victim had started, the assailants should have carried the injured man away and afterwards brought him back to the same spot.

To complicate the situation still more, a thin trail of blood, that had not been noticed during the hours of darkness, had been traced back from the landing-stage along the shoreward length of the East Pier to a squalid alley known as Jimson's Rents. Here was discovered a large pool of blood over which had been thrown a quantity of sawdust.

Since there was only a one-way trail it was presumed that Tarrant Gunville had been struck down close to the entrance to the alley and had been left lying there for several minutes. He had then been lashed up in a sheet of canvas and carried down to the harbour. In the opinion of the police this was not done with the motive of throwing the victim into the water—his assailants could have done so without going to the trouble and risk of carrying him to the landing-stage—but with the object of placing him on board his yacht.

What, then, was the object of the crime? Certainly not robbery, since they had not taken neither his pocket-book, that contained twelve pounds in notes, nor his purse, that had in it thirty shillings' worth of silver.

The police then examined the yacht, having opened the cabin doors by means of a skeleton key. They found nothing that would provide a motive for the crime.

They then communicated with the Easthaven police to inquire into the victim's antecedents and mode of living. There was nothing to report of an adverse character. Tarrant Gunville, it was stated, was a man of moderate independent means and who lived in a self-contained flat in the residential part of the town. During the summer months he cruised extensively in the *Nut*, mostly single-handed, although on occasions he was accompanied by a well-known local J.P. This gentleman, on being interviewed, declared that he knew very little of Tarrant Gunville except as a keen amateur yachtsman; but to the best of his belief he was of good moral character though apt to be taciturn and rather hot-headed. He could put forward no motive for the murderous assault upon Mr. Gunville, who, as far as he knew, had no enemies.

For reasons best known to themselves—possibly because they hoped to score off their own bat—the Otherport police did not call in New Scotland Yard. They concentrated upon the slender clues at their disposal, trying to trace the ownership of the eyeletted canvas in which the victim had been wrapped. They searched for finger-prints, but owing to the coarse texture of the canvas and possibly to the chance of the assailants wearing gloves, the results were negative.

Then it was discovered that the sawdust used in attempting to cover the pool of blood was that of jarrah wood—a timber of Australian origin and rarely used in this country except in connection with yacht-building. Inquiries were made at the two local yacht yards without success. No craft had been built or repaired in either yard that had jarrah used in the work.

The local sawmills were then visited by the police. The manager remembered having sawn up several planks for a well-known country resident—that was three months ago. He'd remarked to the sawyers on the peculiar odour of the wood as it was being cut, something like the smell of eucalyptus. What was more, the sawdust—a bag of it—had been sold to a butcher in the High Street.

Hot on the trail, a detective-sergeant interviewed the purveyor. Yes, he remembered the sawdust with the peculiar smell. He thought his customers wouldn't like the odour if the stuff were sprinkled on the floor of his shop, so he had ordered one of his men to take it to the slaughter-house, which was within fifty yards of Jimson's Rents—the place where, in the opinion of the police, Tarrant Gunville had been struck down.

Next they interviewed the slaughter-man—a squat, powerfully built man with shifty eyes—who had been in trouble with the police on several occasions, mostly on account of his violent, quarrelsome nature.

At first the man denied all knowledge of the patch of sawdust found almost outside his door—he lived in one of the tumble-down houses in Jimson's Rents—but afterwards volunteered a statement.

As usual he had got up at five that morning to get the slaughter-house ready, and as he was going out of the house he nearly stepped into a pool of blood. He had no idea that it was human blood and thought it might be that of a cat. He remembered hearing a cat squeal as if seized by a dog. He had a dog of his own, and in case the animal should get out and lap the stuff, he went to the slaughter-house, filled a bucket with the queer-smelling sawdust and sprinkled the pool.

He was ready to take his oath that he'd gone home at ten on the previous night and hadn't left till the next morning at five. His wife would corroborate the statement.

Asked what time it was he heard the cat squeal, he thought it must have been about eleven o'clock, just as he was going to bed. He couldn't be sure where the noise came from. It might have been from the alley or from the yard at the back of the house.

Had he noticed the pool of blood when he arrived home that night at ten? No, because it was too dark to see anything much. Had his dog barked during the night? It might have done, but as he was a heavy sleeper the slaughter-man would not have paid any attention.

" I'm afraid we've been following a false trail, Rogerson!" observed the Superintendent.

" I'm afraid we have, sir," admitted Detective Sergeant Rogerson sadly.

"Queer doings over yonder," observed Mr. "Bungs" Cotter when Rod and Ned went over to his yard to inspect the damage done to the *Venture*. "Strange, I didn't hear anything till this morning. 'Twere lucky for that gentleman I'd lent you that dinghy o' mine or he might be lying on the bottom of the harbour without anyone knowing anything about it, 'cept the fellows who did the dirty business, for the next eight days!"

"I suppose it was a good thing we happened to be around," admitted Ron.

"First you saves his little yacht by towin' her in and then you saves his life, in a manner o' speaking. Well, strange things happen at sea and stranger ones in port: that's my experience after twenty-one years in the Navy. But I suppose you ain't here to talk about that, but to see what can be done to the *Venture*?"

"Yes; what do you make of her?" asked Ron anxiously, for now that Mr. Gunville had more or less faded out of the picture the fulfilment of his promise to provide the Troop with a larger and better motor cruiser seemed as far off as the poles. They would have to make the best with the *Venture* if she were capable of being reconditioned. In any case, the repairs could not be effected much before the end of August, which meant that there would be no cruising in her during the present holidays.

Old Bungs shook his head dolefully.

"Don't go much on her!" he replied bluntly. "They put elm stringers into her, too. They're rotten through and through. How old did the man who sold her to you say she was?"

"Twelve years!"

The boat-builder snorted.

"Twelve years? Call it twenty-four and you'll be nearer the mark. Transom's clean gone, so that knocks out one part of the evidence. You know all these ex-Naval boats carry their birth certificates?"

"No, I didn't," admitted the Patrol-leader. "Did you, Ned?"

The Second shook his head.

"Well, then, they do," continued Mr. Cotter. "It's carved deep on the inside of the transom and on the side of the stem-head, although the chap who sold her took good care to putty the marks up! See here."

He pointed to the side of the stem-post,

from which he had scraped nearly half a dozen layers of paint, leaving exposed the lettering, DEV.1915.

"There you are!" he declared. "Built at Devonport the second year of the First World War. Put unseasoned wood into her, though I allow the teak's sound enough, and she's eaten up wi' dry rot! Better sell her as she stands, for what she'll fetch!"

Ron and his chum weren't in a position to decide. The *Venture* was the property of the Troop, and until Mr. Dyson was informed and the matter put to the others, no decision could be made.

Two days passed without any fresh development concerning the cowardly attack on Tarrant Gunville. He was not making satisfactory progress, and was still unable to receive visitors.

Meanwhile the police were a bit worried concerning the *Nut*. They didn't want to have to look after her. Neither did the Customs authorities, who seemed to have lost all their former interest both in the yacht and in her owner. The Harbour Master also pointed out that she could not lie alongside the pontoon indefinitely, as it was intended primarily as a landing-stage for dinghies.

The Superintendent of Police had an idea that would relieve him of all responsibility in the matter. Why not get the Sea Scouts to take the yacht away and look after her until her owner was fit and well again?

Ron Bradley, when the proposition was put before him, did not hesitate. Here was a chance of doing a practical Good Turn for the man who had promised them their new motor cruiser.

Within an hour of the Superintendent's request being received, the *Nut* was towed to moorings almost underneath the windows of the Otherport Troop's guard-ship, and arrangements were made to air the sails, ventilate the cabin and to keep the yacht tidy.

Tarrant Gunville had declined to add to his first statement on the attack. He stuck to his words that he hadn't left the East Pier before he was struck down and, most emphatically, he knew nothing of having been lying in a pool of blood in Jimson's Rents.

Yet he was obviously worried about something, and this state of mind, according to the hospital staff, was retarding his recovery. But when one of the nurses, whose cousin was in the Sea Scouts, mentioned to him that the *Nut* was in charge of the Otherport Troop, Tarrant Gunville seemed to take a turn for the better. So much so, that by the end of the next week he was allowed to receive visitors.

Ron and Ned were the first to see the patient, having been enjoined not to remain more than ten minutes.

"It's jolly good of you fellows to keep an eye on the *Nut*," observed Mr. Gunville. "That's two Good Turns you've done me, and so far I've done nothing in return except broken my promise to look in at your—your——"

"Guard-ship, sir," added the Patrol-leader. "Only, it isn't a ship but a loft over the rope-walk."

"I see! A rose by any other name, eh? But having done two Good Turns, would you care to perform another?"

"It depends upon whether we are able," replied Ron guardedly. "You see, every one of us tries to do one Good Turn every day."

"So I've been given to understand," observed the patient whimsically. "It's the *Nut* that's still worrying me. I shan't be able to sail her back to Easthaven, because as soon as I leave here I'm going to some friends in Surrey to recuperate. Her cruising policy ends on the thirteenth of September and I'm most anxious to get her back to her home port well before then. Do you think you Sea Scouts could do this for me?"

The chums looked at one another.

"Wouldn't we just, sir!" exclaimed Ron. "But there may be difficulties with the Association."

"What Association?"

"The Boy Scouts'," explained Ron. "We

would have to get special permission from the District Commissioner before making that longish trip. We'd take it on in a jiffey if we had the chance!"

"Why not ask Mr. Dyson, Ron?" suggested Ned.

"Who's Mr. Dyson?"

"Our Scoutmaster, sir. I thought I'd told you. He's here in this hospital, recovering from an operation."

"I hope you will be able to sail the *Nut* round," said Mr. Gunville. "Then I can write to the shipyard at Easthaven and ask them to get the *Dark Secret* ready for you."

"*Dark Secret*, sir?"

"Yes, that's the name of the motor-cruiser I'm handing over to your Troop. I fancy that name isn't very popular with the Easthaven branch of Her Majesty's Excise and Customs Department! And, by the by, has friend Badger ceased to badger?"

"He hasn't been on board the *Nut* since the night when——"

"When I had a slight and one-sided argument with a rubber truncheon? Ah! Here's my wardress! It would seem that the time is come to say *au revoir*!"

The smiling nurse held the door open in a way that could not be misunderstood.

The two Sea Scouts then were escorted to the private ward where Mr. Dyson, who was now able to sit up in an arm-chair, greeted them warmly.

"Another fortnight, lads, and I'll be back at the Den!" he declared. "Well, what's the news?"

They told him of their visit to Tarrant Gunville.

"As soon as I can get about I'll look him up," said the Scoutmaster. "Perhaps he'll be on his pins before I am. All the same, I'm not so sure about his invitation to you to take the *Nut* back to Easthaven. If I were fit it would be a different matter."

"I could navigate her there, sir!"

"I've no doubt about that, Ron! But, you see, there's the responsibility, borne not entirely by you but by those authorized to give you the necessary permission. Seventy miles is a long way, especially if it means a beat to wind'ard."

"She has a small motor," announced Ned.

"Has she?" rejoined Mr. Dyson. "Then, that being so, why did Mr. Gunville ask for a tow?"

Neither of the two youths could offer any suggestion, until Ned opined that since the engine developed only three and a half horsepower it was insufficient to drive the yacht, with the windage of her lofty Bermudan mast, against the hard wind.

"We were doing only about two knots

until we rounded the West Rat's Tail buoy," added Ron.

Mr. Dyson left it at that for the present; but he had made up his mind to ask Gunville about it.

"I'll write to the Group S.M. and see what he thinks about it," he observed. "The offer of the *Dark Secret* is a generous one, but we mustn't hold the Movement up to severe criticism through a disaster to some of our Troop. We'll leave it at that."

"I don't quite follow, sir," said Ron.

"Well, then, supposing you had permission to take the *Nut* to Easthaven, and a gale sprang up while you were miles from the nearest harbour. The yacht might be swamped and her crew lost. Wouldn't there be an outcry against those who allowed the *Nut* to sail?"

"There might be," agreed the Patrol-leader guardedly. "But, when all's said and done, there are risks in almost every undertaking. The world would be a pretty dull place if there weren't."

"I quite agree," rejoined Mr. Dyson. "But there's this to be considered: you may be quite willing to run certain risks in taking Gunville's yacht round to Easthaven; your crew might be equally ready to share those risks. But what if, through an error of judgment on your part, something goes wrong and some of the crew lose their lives? You'd feel it for the rest of your life. But, mind you, I'm not putting obstacles in your way."

"Then you'll try to get the necessary permission, sir?"

"I'll do my best," replied the S.M. "But I doubt whether I'll succeed."

Mr. Dyson's surmise proved to be correct. In spite of Ron Bradley's qualifications to take charge of a craft, the permission was refused on similar grounds to those put forward by him. But—and that was the liberal coating of sugar to the pill—the *Nut* could be taken to her home port by a crew of Otherport Sea Scouts provided a fully qualified Scoutmaster accompanied them.

The Seagulls held a pow-pow and discussed the proposition. Had Mr. Dyson been fit and well they would have welcomed his presence on board; but a strange S.M.? It was something of a gamble; and where was a Scoutmaster to be found who would have to desert his own Troop for the time being and spend a week or more in the necessary cramped quarters of a little yacht of under ten tons' displacement?

The Sea Scouts were in the midst of their deliberations when Group S.M. Miles arrived at the guard-ship.

"Excuse me butting in, you fellows!" he exclaimed; "but I've had a note from Dyson, from which I gather you're in a slight difficulty."

"We are, sir!" agreed Ron.

"Then let me help you out of it. Rules and regulations are framed to be carried out; if they aren't, it reflects discredit both upon those who make them and those who break them. You fellows have a chance of a topping holiday afloat, especially in view of the fact that you've had a mishap with your own craft. My suggestion is this—and you are quite at liberty to turn it down if you want—that I go with you in nominal charge. You'll carry on just as if I weren't there, except"—he added with a humorous smile—"I'd like to grub with you, since I'm precious little use at preparing my own meals! Otherwise you'll sail and work the yacht, with your patrol-leader as skipper, and I'll sit back and not interfere, unless you ask for my advice, or I consider that it's necessary in the interests of all concerned that I should have to butt in. Is that clear?"

There was no hesitation about the Seagulls' reply. Previously they had been a little awed of Mr. Peter Miles. He seemed to have been on a higher plane, but now, in the midst of their difficulties, he had voluntarily offered to step into Mr. Dyson's shoes, as it were, and had gone even further: he had left the Patrol with practically a free hand.

"Thanks awfully, sir!" they exclaimed in unison.

"Then that's that!" declared Mr. Miles cheerfully. "I'll get the necessary permission. To let you into a secret, I've arranged for that already! So all you have to do is to fix your sailing date, and Peter Miles will duly report on board as super-cargo!"

CHAPTER X

THE TRIAL TRIP

It wasn't quite so easy as that!

The *Nut* had to be provisioned and made ready for sea. Her sails and standing and running gear had to be overhauled, the auxiliary motor had to be examined and given a trial.

As Ron remarked, it would be silly to make a start and then have to put back because of some slight defect that ought to have been spotted before they left Otherport Harbour.

One of the chief items was the cost of provisioning the yacht. The crew fully expected that Mr. Gunville would make a contribution towards this, since, to his undisguised satisfaction, they were undertaking the trip principally on his behalf. Quite possibly, in his present state, the thought hadn't entered his head, so the Sea Scouts had to make their own arrangements.

Georgie Hughes, in addition to "signing-on" in his usual capacity as cook, volunteered to act as messman. Each of the crew contributed towards the cost of the provisions, either in money or kind or both—and their parents " weighed in " most generously.

Mr. Moore, Christie's father, for example, gave a hundredweight of potatoes and four seven-pound airtight tins filled with flour—a gift that made " Cookie " have visions of spending the whole of his time in the galley. By way of contrast, Mrs. Anderson, Wee Jock's mother, contributed four pounds of home-made jam.

From Mr. Coleman, who ran a garage in Otherport, came four tins of petrol and two gallons of paraffin, together with a verbal caution against the risk of fire and the hope that none of the crew would smoke and drop lighted cigarette ends into the bilges! But, of course, Sea Scouts wouldn't do that sort of thing!

At length the day arrived for the trial run. It was a perfect sailing morning, with a steady sou'westerly breeze. The tide, an hour after full, was setting out of the harbour at about one and a half knots.

Musty had given the motor a run, but rather to his disappointment the Patrol-leader decided to beat out under sail, just to give the idlers on the pier an idea of how a yacht could be handled without mechanical aid.

" You all know your various jobs!" he addressed the crew. " We'll have the staysail up first, then cast off the mooring. As soon as we're under way up goes the mainsail, and we'll sail close hauled out of the harbour. All ready?"

Ron gave the first order, and before the headsail could be sheeted home the mooring buoy was thrown overboard.

Then, as soon as the Bermudan mainsail was hoisted, he put the helm down and had the mainsheet hauled well in.

He had a shock!

Instead of going about with the ease and grace expected of a craft of her lines and rig, the *Nut* began to behave like an obstinate mule.

Very slowly she came into the wind, with her canvas slatting violently in the fresh breeze. Then, instead of paying off on the other tack, she lost way and began to drift stern foremost.

The *Nut* was " in irons ", one of the most awkward situations in which a sailing craft can find herself, especially in a crowded harbour.

She certainly was in a tight fix. If she could pay off and gather way on either tack, she would be foul of either of the two large yachts that had come in only that morning. If she carried sternway much longer, she would drift across the hawse of a large tramp, the crew of which were watching with amused interest the plight of the *Nut*.

Luckily Ron kept his head.

" Down headsail!" he ordered, followed by " Let go!"

Promptly Lofty dropped the anchor over the bows, checking the fiercely running cable when some twelve fathoms of chain had followed the " hook ". By this time the staysail was down and muzzled.

The *Nut* brought up with a decided jerk, with her counter within ten feet of the tramp steamer's bows, and, happily, the anchor held.

The danger averted, the crew looked at their youthful skipper and waited for his explanation.

Ron could give none, although he had an idea that the yacht had fouled some light moorings and was towing them through the soft mud on the bed of the harbour.

It was disconcerting—humiliating. The crews of the two large yachts were still standing by with fenders ready to ward off the worst of a collision; the hands of the tramp were chaffing the Sea Scouts and offering them ribald advice; while on shore the usual crowd of loungers had sat up and taken notice of the fact that the *Nut* was in trouble again.

Ron recalled that he'd never seen the *Nut* under sail. Perhaps she was what seamen term an " old cow " when under canvas, and that was the reason why Tarrant Gunville had got into difficulties before the *Venture* took the yacht in tow.

The only thing to be done, it seemed, was to lower the mainsail and get the *Nut* back to her temporary moorings by means of the engine.

Once more, troubles did not come singly; for when the crew attempted to lower the canvas the peak dropped a few feet and obstinately refused to budge. This was bad enough, but it would have been far worse—positively dangerous—if the yacht had been struck by a heavy squall when standing out to sea.

It occurred to Ron that Tarrant Gunville had proposed that the Sea Scouts should take the *Nut* out, knowing that she was a cranky craft, with the deliberate idea of courting disaster. Perhaps she was heavily insured, and the owner hoped to reap pecuniary gain out of her loss!

"Hello, you fellows!" hailed a voice. "Can I bear a hand?"

Unnoticed by the crew, a dinghy had come alongside. In her was a pleasant-faced yachtsman from one of the nearby craft.

"We can't stow the mainsail," confessed Ron.

"When was it last set?"

The Patrol-leader had to think before he replied. The sail had been aired on several occasions since the Sea Scouts had taken charge of the yacht, but never had it been hoisted right up.

"Not for the last fortnight, sir!"

"Then it's not to be wondered at," rejoined the newcomer, as he made the dinghy's painter fast. "Grease, my lad, grease! That's what's wanted. A touch of grease is worth half a ton of beef!"

"I don't quite understand," said Ron.

"You know what 'putting more beef into it' means? It means letting brawn and muscle tackle a job when a little grease will do the trick. Your trouble is that the main track, being brass, has corroded a little through salt air. I'll set that right."

The Good Samaritan had come armed with a rag smothered with grease. Agilely he made his way aloft until he gained the spreaders. In a couple of minutes, having lubricated the track, he bade the Sea Scouts lower away.

The mainsail came down perfectly.

"She seemed frightfully sluggish when you tried to tack," observed the yachtsman, when he regained the deck. "I thought you'd given us a clout."

"So did I," admitted Ron frankly.

"That's all I can do for you," continued their benefactor. "I know something about yachts, although a fellow's education in that line is never complete. There's always something fresh to learn."

" We'll start the motor and get back to our moorings," said the Patrol-leader, after the yachtsman had rowed away. " Blest if I know what's wrong with her."

" Say, Skipper!" exclaimed Musty, pointing to a lever under the stern-bench, " did you touch that?"

" No; why?"

" Someone has! Accidentally perhaps; but if I'd started up the engine, she'd have gone ahead and hit something. She hasn't a reverse, you know."

The engine was fitted with a folding propeller that, when not in use, was closed something like an umbrella, so as to offer little or no resistance when the yacht was under sail. For some reason the blades were extended and in consequence would greatly check the craft's speed.

" It's jammed!" declared Musty, after attempting to thrust the lever back. " Must have fouled something!"

Ron and Ned leant over the short counter. To their surprise they discovered that the propeller was not only unfolded, but had hanging on to it a rope attached to a large canvas sack! Had the engine been started, the rope would have wound itself round the propeller and, as likely as not, the *Nut* would have had to be put ashore before the obstruction could be removed.

As it was, the sack, acting as a sort of sea-anchor while the yacht was moving through the water, had been solely responsible for the *Nut's* sluggishness.

With the aid of a boathook the canvas was removed. It proved to be an old coaling sack that had caught in the stationary blades of the propeller.

"That's our trouble!" declared Ned. "Now, Ron, let's see how she handles now!"

Again sail was hoisted and the anchor brought on board, fortunately without having fouled any of the numerous moorings lying on the bed of the harbour.

This time the *Nut* handled magnificently, turning to wind'ard with the greatest ease. It didn't take the helmsman long to "get the hang of things" nor the crew to handle unaccustomed sheets.

Two hours later, drenched with spray yet supremely happy, the Sea Scouts brought the little craft faultlessly into harbour. They were delighted by the ease with which the yacht handled and with which the towering mass of canvas could be lowered.

They rowed ashore by relays in the diminutive canvas dinghy. Mr. Miles was awaiting them on the pier.

"You brought her in splendidly," he declared.

"It was a good thing you didn't see us get

under way, sir!" confessed Ron. "We made a bit of a mess of things!"

"How?" asked the G.S.M.

The Patrol-leader explained.

"As long as one knows what is wrong and can make things good there's no harm done, but experience gained," remarked Mr. Miles reflectively. "We're starting—when?"

"At nine to-morrow, sir; the east-going stream starts at nine-thirty."

"Good! Everything on board? Now, I think it would be a good idea if some of you sleep aboard to-night."

"We can manage that; can't we, Ned?" asked Ron. "Any particular reason, sir?"

Peter Miles told him.

CHAPTER XI

INTRUDERS

"It's going to be a tight squeeze, old son!" remarked Ned, when he and Ron boarded the *Nut* just before seven in the evening, accompanied by Nick, a nondescript terrier belonging to the Patrol-leader.

"What is?" asked the Patrol-leader.

"Sleeping eight of us on board," replied the Second. "There are two settees in this saloon, two cot-bunks in the for'ard cabin and two more in the fo'c'sle. That makes sleeping accommodation for six; where do the extra two fellows turn in?"

"On the floor!" was the reply. "It's only a two days' run and that means just one night afloat. If we can't stick a little discomfort we aren't Sea Scouts! For that matter, we could take turn about!"

"How about Mr. Miles?"

"He'll fit in all right," declared Ron cheerfully. "He knows what the accommodation's like. He told me he could sleep on a clothes-line and put up with anything on board except cooking his own grub! He'll be the last to grumble, I guess. Now, what berth are you taking yourself?"

This point having been settled, the chums unstowed their gear and placed their blankets on their respective bunks. The dog was given an old rug and told to lie down on the floor of the saloon.

"He's been fed," announced Ron, in reply to his chum's inquiry. "But I'll put a bowl of water for him in case the beggar's thirsty. Unless he's disturbed you won't know he's on board!"

Almost at once came a slight bump on the yacht's side, the sound being magnified when heard from within. Nick stood up, with hair bristling, and gave a low, almost inaudible growl.

The two lads hurried out to the cockpit and looked around. They found nothing to cause alarm. A gentle breeze had sprung up and, since there was no tide running, the canvas dinghy had been blown alongside and was bumping lightly against the yacht's top-sides.

"If that goes on all night we won't get much sleep," declared Ned, who knew the vagaries of dinghies. "Let's haul her on board."

It was the work of a few minutes to lift the dinghy out of the water, fold her flat and stow her on deck inside the starboard shrouds. Then the chums, having made all snug below, turned in, although it was now only nine o'clock. They were anticipating a heavy day on the morrow.

The *Nut*, lying in the upper part of the harbour, had a snug berth and was well out of the way of traffic. In consequence, it was not necessary to hoist a riding-light as would have been the case had she been brought-up nearer the fairway. Until the electric lamps on the quays were extinguished at midnight she was plainly visible in the steely blue glare they cast.

It seemed to Ron that he hadn't been asleep more than a few minutes before he was awakened by Nick giving another low growl.

Checking his natural instinct to order the dog to "keep quiet and go to sleep", and to settle down himself, the Patrol-leader sat up and listened intently through the open scuttle. It was pitch dark, with the exception of the green lamps that marked the landing steps at the upper quay, so he knew that it was now after midnight.

As Ron listened, he felt the yacht heel slightly to port. The heeling was not caused, he realized, by the swell of a passing craft since the *Nut* did not swing back to starboard; nor, unless she had dragged her ground tackle, could she be aground, since the moorings were laid in nine feet of water at ordinary low spring tide.

Someone had come on board, and whoever he might be, he was under the mistaken impression that the *Nut* was deserted.

Slipping out of his bunk, Ron clasped his chum's hand, softly, yet maintaining a firm, gentle pressure—a sure means of waking the soundest sleeper without the risk of causing him to start or call out.

Ned was on his feet in a couple of seconds without making a sound.

Both lads waited, listening intently. The deck beams creaked under the weight of the intruder.

Then they heard a voice speaking.

"Laced!" it whispered.

"Cut it adrift, then," rejoined a companion, who, judging by the sounds, was in a boat alongside.

Ron guessed rightly that for some reason the midnight marauders were about to remove the sail cover, possibly with the idea of stealing the mainsail.

Mr. Miles had warned him that *perhaps* there would be an attempt at sabotage; that some persons, having a grudge or a grievance against Tarrant Gunville, would do something that would either prevent the *Nut* from leaving Otherport or would disable her when she was on her voyage. Without the shadow of a doubt, it seemed to the listeners, the Group S.M.'s suspicions were being proved just.

Having groped for his torch, Ron crept to the cabin doors, which were ajar but not locked.

"Ready?" he whispered.

"Right!" replied Ned.

The Patrol-leader pushed open the doors, making as much noise as he could.

"Rats! Seize 'em, Nick! Get 'em, boy!" he shouted.

It was almost his undoing, for in his excitement the terrier dashed past the Patrol-leader's bare legs, almost throwing him off his feet.

Out into the cockpit the dog flew like an arrow from a bow. There he stopped, spun round, and with a single bound jumped on to the cabin top.

Before the intruders knew what was happening, Nick went into effective action. He went straight for the fellow who had apparently begun to cut away the sail cover and bit hard at the leg of his trousers. It was a generous mouthful, since it took in a portion of the fellow's calf.

Without giving a thought for his companion and the trouble he was in, the man in the boat pushed off. Even as he did so the fellow on board jumped for it, with the intention of landing in the boat, while Nick continued to hang on to his trousers like grim death.

Dazzled by the beam of the Patrol-leader's

G 715

INTRUDERS BY NIGHT

Page 110

torch, and hampered by the weight of the dog, the wretched fellow miscalculated his distance and dropped with a tremendous splash into the water.

This was more than Ron had expected or wished.

The tide was running strongly. His pet was in the harbour and the dinghy in its collapsed state was stowed on deck, by no means ready for aiding in a rescue.

Although the terrier generally held on to whatever he gripped, his sudden immersion proved to be too much for his tenacity. He came to the surface clear of the man, who was swimming after the boat and alternately cursing his companion for deserting him and imploring him to stop and pick him up.

Having repulsed the invaders, Ron's thoughts were centred upon his dog. The animal was swimming hard towards the yacht's counter, for already he had been swept astern by the strong ebb, but very soon it was evident that Nick was making no progress. Actually he was being carried slowly yet surely away, and unless something could be done he would be swept down the harbour, between the pier-heads, to the open sea.

By the time the dinghy could be opened out and launched the animal would be lost to sight in the darkness.

Only for an instant did Ron hesitate. Handing Ned his torch, he picked up a coil of grass rope lying in the counter, made one end fast to the horse and, grasping the other end, dived overboard.

Luckily the coils did not kink. A few strokes brought him within reach of the strongly swimming Nick. He grasped the dog by the scruff of his neck just as a disconcerting jerk told the lad that the grass rope had been paid out to its fullest extent. He was only just in time!

"Heave on, Ned!" shouted the Patrol-leader, contenting himself by hanging on to the rope with one hand and to the dog with the other.

Planting his feet firmly against the after-coaming of the cockpit, Ned hauled away and was surprised to find how much strength was required. It had never occurred to him before how strong the ebb tide could be. Hand over hand he brought the warp inboard. It required as much exertion as if he had to swarm up a rope; but at length he could discern his chum's face through the darkness.

A few feet more and Ron was able to grasp one of the fenders. Ned leant over the side and relieved his chum of his burden.

Nick promptly went below and shook himself, shedding showers of water over his master's and Ned's bunks with the utmost impartiality!

Unaided, the Patrol-leader was unable to haul himself on deck. The exertion had well-nigh deprived him of breath, and not until Ned had made a bowline with which his chum could obtain a foothold, was Ron able to draw himself clear of the water.

By this time the sound of oars had died away. The miscreants were already on shore, their plan frustrated.

Shedding his saturated pyjamas, Ron retired to his cabin to dry himself before turning in again. Ned followed, not noticing in the darkness that the grass rope in which he had made the bowline was quietly slipping over the stern, owing to the drag of the tide.

"I wonder what those fellows—" began Ned; then: "I say, does the cabin roof leak? My bunk's sopping!"

"So's mine! It's Nick: he's been shaking himself!"

"*Nut* ahoy!"

The hail brought the two Sea Scouts out into the cockpit again.

Approaching could be seen the red and green navigation lamps of a motor launch.

"Motor boat ahoy!" replied Ron.

"We're coming alongside!" continued the voice, which the Sea Scouts now recognized as that of the efficient Mr. Badger.

"Fenders out, Ned!" ordered the Patrol-leader.

The visiting craft was only about ten yards away when her engine stopped abruptly. She was still carrying way, but would have failed to come alongside had not one of her crew thrown a rope.

The Sea Scouts hauled her nearer until her bows were level with the yacht's cockpit. The object of the Customs visit was for the time being not under consideration. Mr. Badger and the two boatmen who made up the launch's crew were arguing as to the cause of the motor's sudden stoppage.

"It's something round the prop, sir!" declared one of Mr. Badger's minions. "Clutch free and she starts. Put her ahead or astern and she pulls up dead!"

To confirm his assertion the man prodded overside with a boat-hook. Almost at once he hooked part of a grass warp.

"Sort of thing blighters like that would do," grumbled Mr. Badger. "Cut it—cut it as close to the propeller as you can. She may free herself then."

Out came the man's knife. It took three slashes to sever the rope. One end floated clear and was lost to sight in the darkness.

"It's no use, sir!" declared the other boatman, who was in charge of the engine. "She won't take it. There'll be fathoms of rope wound round the blade and the shaft, I'll allow!"

Mr. Badger said things under his breath, but soon realized that, although he might be letting off steam, he was not contributing anything to mend matters. He hadn't come alongside the *Nut* at one o'clock in the morning for nothing!

"Hello, you there!" he greeted the Sea Scouts. "What's been the matter with you?"

"Two men came aboard and started to cut away the mainsail cover, sir!" reported Ron. "They got away."

"Pity! We were all ready to nab them. Did you see what they were like?"

"No, it was too dark, but Nick got hold of one all right!" said the Patrol-leader.

"And didn't the fellow yell!" added Ned. "He fell in, and Nick went in holding on to him."

"I hope Nick left his trade-mark!" observed Mr. Badger. "If the victim is a nervous sort of chap he'll go to a doctor or a hospital, and then we may be able to ask him what he has to say for himself. Now I'll come aboard you and have another look round."

He switched on an electric lamp and stepped from the launch into the *Nut's* cockpit; but instead of going below, as Ron expected he would, he went for'ard.

"What's this?" he asked.

"Our canvas dinghy, sir!"

"Oh yes, I remember. Gunville had it

stowed in the for'ard cabin. Sure those fellows didn't touch it?"

" I can't say," replied Ron. " When we came out one of them was busy with the sail-cover."

" Well, he did," declared Mr. Badger, shining the light upon the dinghy. " He's jabbed a hole in it! And, glory be! he's left his knife!"

Apprehensively, Ron made his way along the side deck. Sure enough, he could see a gash, nearly six inches in length, in the canvas close to the keel.

" Why should anyone do such a dirty trick, sir?" asked the Patrol-leader. " We would have found it out directly we launched the dinghy to go ashore. But supposing we were outside and had to use her in a hurry?"

" They're both dirty pieces of work, if you ask me," replied Mr. Badger. " Wouldn't stop at anything. But, of course, this might have been done accidentally when he dropped the knife. Aha! and what's this?"

It was a piece of chequered cloth lying close to one of the main shroud plates.

" We've to thank Nick for that clue, Ron!" exclaimed Ned. " He must have had two goes at the man's leg, since he was hanging on when they both went overboard."

" The piece of stuff and the mark of the dog's teeth are sufficient to identify the fellow," added Mr. Badger. " Not my job, though. I'll have to see the Superintendent of Police about it."

" But I know where that piece of cloth came from, sir!" declared the Patrol-leader. " It's part of the stuff I am using for cleaning the brasswork. I thought I'd put it away with the rest, but it must have caught in that shackle!"

" Confound it!" ejaculated Mr. Badger. " Everything's going wrong! This must be my birthday!"

He flashed the beam of his lantern along the uncovered portion of the boom, which, like those of modern racing yachts, was oval-shaped in section.

" They don't seem to have damaged the sail," he continued. " Well, I'll be getting along. It'll mean putting the launch on the slip to get that prop clear! Now, you youngsters, you'd better turn in. I don't think you'll be disturbed again to-night."

" But why did those fellows come down?" asked the Patrol-leader.

Mr. Badger ignored the question. He went back to the launch and ordered his two men to get the oars out.

" He seems a bit peeved!" observed Ron, when the sound of the oars died away in the darkness.

Ned grinned.

" Good thing he didn't tumble to it, old son!"

" Tumble to what?"

" It was our grass rope that fouled the launch's propeller," explained Ned. " Must have trailed overboard after I helped you on board. He blamed the fellows who tried to sneak the mainsail, though I suppose they won't mind that."

" And how about turning in again?" suggested Ron. " It's nearly two o'clock, and we're due to be under way at nine."

CHAPTER XII

NICK WINS HIS WAY

The chums turned out at seven o'clock, to find the sun shining in an unclouded sky and a light breeze ruffling the surface of the harbour.

"Just our luck!" exclaimed Ned. "Wind sou'-west—a dead beat the whole way."

"So much the better," rejoined Ron. "We're in no hurry and, besides, this wind'll go round with the sun. Come on: slap it about! There's a lot to do before the other fellows arrive."

There was! First and foremost, the dinghy had to be repaired. In her present condition she wouldn't keep afloat more than a couple of minutes.

Fortunately the *Nut* was well supplied with bos'un's stores. Cutting a piece of canvas two inches longer and wider than the rent, Ron soaked it in linseed oil and varnish before applying it to the gap in the dinghy. While Ned held it firmly in position, the Patrol-leader sewed it on with bees-waxed twine. The dinghy was then laid flat upon the cabin top so that the sun could get to the oiled patch.

"It'll be dry in an hour, I reckon," declared Ron. "That'll give me time to take Nick home before the others arrive."

"Wish Nick was coming with us," said Ned.

"He'd be sorry for himself if he did. He's always seasick if he goes outside the harbour. Look! There's Mr. Miles and the other chaps! Well, we can't fetch them off."

Balancing himself on the encumbered cabin top, the Patrol-leader semaphored:

"Dinghy leaking. Can you borrow a boat?"

Apparently there was no difficulty about that, for in a few minutes the Sea Scouts were running a tubby dinghy down the slipway and putting their gear into her.

In addition to Mr. Miles, there were four Sea Scouts, one of them a member of the Seal patrol.

"Where's Christie?" shouted Ron as the boat drew within hailing distance.

"Not coming!"

"Where's Wee Jock?"

"His people won't let him come!"

That was disappointing in a way, although Mr. Miles was secretly glad. The yacht would have been uncomfortably crowded with eight on board. He had been anticipating discomfort—it would have been like sardines in a tin—but for the sake of the Patrol he would have put up with it cheerfully.

"You coming, Ginger?"

The Second of the Seals shook his head.

"Wish I were," he replied. "I'm taking the boat back."

"Well, then, you might take Nick with you."

But the dog obstinately declined to be taken. He would have gone readily enough with his owner, but not with anyone else. Backing into a locker large enough to hold him, but only just, he defied Ron's efforts to dislodge him.

"If you can't get him out, Ron, none of us can," said Lofty. "Why not pretend to get into the dinghy. He'll follow: you can nip back and Ginger rows off with the dog!"

"Right-o," agreed the Patrol-leader. "Come on, Nick! All ashore!"

The moment his master stepped into the dinghy Nick was out of his bolt-hole like a flash. Ginger gave one stroke with the oars, and as he did so Ron jumped from the stern-sheets to the *Nut's* waterways.

At least, that was what he intended to do. He had forgotten that his leap would give additional momentum to the comparatively light dinghy. He missed the side of the yacht by a good six inches, and, although he managed to grip the coaming with both hands, that did not prevent him going in up to his neck!

The other fellows yelled with merriment. They simply couldn't help it; neither could

Ron when the humorous side of the affair dawned upon him.

Nick had cleared the intervening distance in a single bound, and now the animal was thrusting his head over the side and frantically licking the face of his almost totally immersed master.

"You'll have to go home and get some dry things now," suggested Ned.

"No fear!" declared Ron. "If I do I'll be told I'm a silly ass to fall overboard and perhaps my people will take the same view as Wee Jock's. Besides, I've more kit on board. So there you are, Nick! You've made up your mind to stay, and if you'll be feeling sorry for yourself you've only yourself to blame!"

Group S.M. Miles, engaged in unpacking his scanty belongings in the fore-cabin, smiled to himself. He was very fond of most dogs, and, by the uncanny instinct possessed by canines, dogs almost invariably took to him. With Nick on board he would no longer be the odd man "out", the self-constituted isolationist.

He was glad that Nick had won his way.

CHAPTER XIII "WE HAVE LETTERS FOR YOU!"

Acting upon the principle that it is better by far to be a few minutes too soon than a second too late, the crew of the *Nut* got under way a quarter of an hour earlier than the arranged time.

Their departure, carried out without any awkward incident, was witnessed by only a few people compared with the curious crowds who often thronged the pier-heads. For one thing, the Sea Scouts' parents and friends found nine in the morning an inconvenient time, while those who composed the usual type of onlookers, the trippers and excursionists, wouldn't start arriving much before noon.

There were, however, some who took more than a passing interest in the *Nut*, as, under whole mainsail and unrolled foresail, she slipped between the pier-heads.

One was Mr. Badger. For several reasons he was glad to see the last of her. He had not gained any *kudos* over his several visits to the yacht, and whatever his suspicions might have been concerning Tarrant Gunville and his little craft, he had not been able to confirm them.

Even the information given him by Mr. Miles, to the effect that he had overheard two strangers declaring their intention of "getting the stuff before she clears out", had led to nothing but a mishap to the Customs launch and a good deal of chaff from his colleagues.

Another spectator, though from afar, was Scoutmaster Dyson, who longingly watched through one of the hospital windows the departure of the *Nut* with one of *his* patrols as crew, but in charge of another S.M. He had trained the lads and now, through no fault of his own, he had been deprived of the fruits of his labours; but that did not prevent him from expressing a wish for the success of their endeavours.

Yet another, and through an adjoining window of the hospital, was Mr. Tarrant Gunville. Still confined to his bed, he had now recovered sufficiently to be propped up with pillows in order to watch his yacht set sail with a crew composed chiefly of mere youths. He, too, was impressed by the smart way in which the *Nut* was being handled. He would be all the more pleased when he received the news that the *Nut* had arrived safely at Easthaven.

From an unfrequented part of the sea wall

two other men followed with their eyes the little yacht as, close-hauled on the port tack, she lifted to the gentle swell of the open sea. One of the men went by the name of Spike Dawkins; the other answered readily enough to Grubber and less readily to his real name of William Gubbins.

It was Spike whom Mr. Miles had overheard making references to "getting the stuff off her", which probably meant stealing the yacht's mainsal either for the purpose of delaying her departure or as a means of adding to their limited financial resources. On the other hand, it might have meant something very different. Had Mr. Miles been able to overhear more of the conversation between these two worthies he would have had food for thought in the veiled reference to "that double-crossing swine", whoever he might be.

As it was, the Group S.M. had passed his information on to Mr. Badger, who, unfortunately, had arrived upon the scene a few minutes too late. Meanwhile Ron and Ned, ably assisted by Nick, had frustrated the nefarious nocturnal designs of Messrs. Spike and Grubber, who, however, had not thrown up the sponge.

Needless to say, Spike and his companion did not give a friendly wave to the departing yacht; instead, after a hurried exchange of views and discussion of plans, they boarded the next motor bus for Dockingham—a small harbour approximately half-way between Otherport and Easthaven.

Oblivious of the two rascals' intentions, the crew of the *Nut* were revelling in the breeze and the bright sunshine as the yacht, close-hauled, was making steady progress toward her destination.

It was one of those perfect sailing days when a weather-going tide and a steady breeze make a beat to wind'ard one of the most pleasurable thrills that can fall to the lot of a keen yachtsman.

With her lee rail just awash, her generous spread of canvas drawing without the suspicion of a shake, and the wind twanging the tautened weather shrouds like harp strings, the *Nut* was making a good five knots.

Everything seemed just perfect!

On deck Ned was at the helm, with Musty and Lofty sitting at their ease in the cockpit. Georgie Hughes was below, busily preparing the first meal of the voyage; Ron, as navigator, was writing up the log and plotting the *Nut's* position on the chart, the latter merely as a matter of form since he knew the coast intimately as far east as Dockingham. The log, of course, was a different matter, since it had to be submitted for inspection and report after the termination of the voyage.

Nick, none too happy, was coiled up on the Patrol-leader's bunk.

Ron was not the only one busy with paper and pencil below. Alone in the fore-cabin, Mr. Miles was wrestling with a number of " returns " required by headquarters. It was a good opportunity to get down to it, and as he tackled a pile of documents that had an irritating tendency to roll off the table as the yacht heeled, he found himself wondering how many Scouts realize the amount of paper work that, unseen by them, goes on for their welfare and for the successful continuance of the Movement.

" Motor cruiser on our port bow, Skipper!" announced Ned, giving the P.L. the title that was by rights the absent Mr. Dyson's. " She's signalling us!"

Ron came on deck and saw that Lofty was taking the message, which was being sent out by means of hand flags by a man standing precariously on the chart-house roof of the craft in question.

" Wants us to close with her," announced Lofty. " She's sprung a leak!"

" Very good!" rejoined the Patrol-leader. " We'll make one more board and then heave-to under her lee and see what's to be done. Stand by to go about!"

The *Nut* went about on the other tack without the slightest hesitation—a contrast to her unfortunate manœuvres in Otherport Harbour. Judging his distance admirably, Ron ordered the headsail to wind'ard and the mainsail to be well sheeted home. Hove-to, she lost way about twenty yards from the stationary motor cruiser, the engine of which was pumping a steady stream of water from the bilges.

"Are you wanting assistance?" asked Ron. "We saw you signalling."

"Yes and no," replied the owner. "We can keep the leak under control and turn back for Otherport. But what's worrying us is the fact that we've letters, parcels and newspapers for the Lone Bull Lighthouse. If you could take them out for us we'd be greatly obliged."

It was a reasonable request. The Lone Bull was about eight miles away, bearing east by south, and in any case the *Nut* would have to pass within a mile or so of it. Although the leak in the motor cruiser was stated to be not serious it might increase, so that the sooner she made Otherport—the nearest harbour—where the defects could be made good, the better.

"Certainly, sir!" agreed Ron. "Overboard with the dinghy, smartly, lads!" ("I hope that patch will hold!" he added, under his breath.)

"Belay there!" hailed the owner of the motor cruiser. "We'll send our dinghy. Don't trouble to launch yours!"

In a very short space of time the dinghy

was swung outboard and lowered. Into her dropped one of the crew, followed by four sacks stuffed to overflowing.

" That's the lot!" declared the yacht hand with a cheerful grin, having pulled across, as he transferred the consignment for the lighthouse to the *Nut's* cockpit. " The guv'nor's very anxious to get it delivered, but 'tain't wise to keep out when the old hooker's making five gallons a minute."

" What started the leak?" asked the P.L. " Though perhaps you don't know."

" Bumped against a bit o' wreckage, I'll allow," explained the man. " I was down below at the time, but it fetched me on deck in a brace o' shakes! We found she'd started a butt against her forefoot, but I reckon if we don't press her too much we'll keep the leak well under, unless it gets worse."

The dinghy returned to her parent ship. After an exchange of farewells, the *Nut* let her sails draw, while the motor cruiser, with her engines running at quarter-throttle, made off in the opposite direction.

Mr. Miles, who had witnessed the incident from the saloon, returned to the fore-cabin. From what he had seen he could only feel increased confidence in the capabilities of the youthful crew. The way in which they had hove-to would have satisfied the most exacting critic.

" If we were to do the thing properly we should be flying a white burgee with a bugle on it," observed Lofty.

" What does that mean?" asked George, who had come out into the cockpit to heave a pail of slush overboard.

" That we're carrying Her Majesty's mails," replied Lofty. " As it is, we'll have to hoist the signal: ' I have letters for you ', when we sight the Lone Bull."

" Won't that cause a sensation amongst the lighthouse keepers!" remarked Musty. " Is the lighthouse in sight yet?"

" Yes, the upper part is showing above the horizon," replied Lofty, after scanning the skyline with his binoculars. " You're almost dead on it, Ned. You may fetch it on this tack if the tide continues in our favour."

" The wind's veered during the last half-hour," rejoined Ned. " If it goes on doing it we'll fetch the Lone Bull easily on this tack."

Ned proved to be right. The wind became more and more free; it became necessary to free sheets and slacken away the lee-runners. But, with the shift of wind and the sea becoming stronger towards midday, the breeze fell light.

" Hadn't I better start the motor?" asked Musty eagerly.

" No jolly fear!" replied Ron. " This is a

full-powered sailing yacht, and while there's enough wind to give her steerage way we're sailing. After all, what's the hurry?"

The question was unanswerable. The longer the voyage lasted, within certain limits, the more pleasure the Seagulls would get out of it. The Patrol-leader was determined to make the passage under sail, only resorting to the motor in case of a prolonged calm or with a similar good excuse.

Gradually the lighthouse rose higher and higher until the whole of the tower of white stone, with two red bands and capped by the imposing lantern, stood out clearly against the dark-blue sky. For eighty or a hundred yards north and south ran ledges of sinister black rocks against which the sea was breaking heavily, and through which rushed masses of dazzling white foam that contrasted vividly with the background of sky.

Although the Lone Bull Lighthouse warned mariners to keep off—either by its powerful light at night or by its strident-voiced siren in foggy weather—the Sea Scouts were closing with it. They knew what liberties they could take with those formidable rocks and where and how far they could go with a reasonable margin of safety.

Half-way up the leach of the *Nut's* mainsail flew the two-flag signal that told the lighthouse keepers they would soon be in actual and material contact with the outside world. From the flagstaff by the side of the gallery fluttered the "acknowledgment", and presently two men emerged from a doorway some fifty feet above the base of the tower and descended a vertical iron ladder to the weed-covered rocks.

It was now a quarter ebb, so the two lighthouse keepers, scrambling over the weed-covered rocks, came down to the landing-place—a narow gulley bounded on both sides by a natural causeway.

"By the mark, three!" announced Musty, who, being debarred from his usual job of engineer, was engaged in the task of swinging the lead.

"Down helm! In staysail!" ordered Ron, and as the yacht, with mainsail a-flutter, lost way: "Let go!"

Soon the *Nut* was riding gently to ten fathoms of cable with her anchor buoyed and in calm water under the lee of the rocks. The mainsail was lowered and roughly stowed, and then the dinghy was opened and dropped over the side. To everyone's satisfaction, she was as tight as a bottle.

"You'd better take the stuff ashore, Ned," suggested the Patrol-leader.

Deeply though not dangerously laden, the canvas cockleshell made for the landing-place.

" Glad to see you, Ned!" was the senior keeper's greeting. " You've got a new craft this time?"

" She's not ours," explained Ned. " We're taking her round to Easthaven. The motor cruiser that was bringing your letters sprang a leak and her skipper asked us to bring them along. You've a big batch of papers and things!"

" They're not all letters and newspapers," explained the man, who, like his two companions, lived at Otherport when duty did not call him to the lonely outpost. " Mr. Osborne, that's the owner of the craft, sends us parcels—baccy and such like. He's done so for years, ever since Joe Barnes, my opposite number, found him on the rocks just along there, on a foggy November night. The wreck of his old craft is still to be seen—at least the keel and a few timbers. Now you're here, would you care to look over the lighthouse?"

" Sorry, but I can't wait," replied the Sea Scout. " We want to make Dockingham Roads by sunset."

" You'll do it easily enough and with plenty of time to spare. Tide's against you and the east-going stream won't make till after six, so you won't gain much with the wind as it is, until then. Get the other fellows ashore. The yacht won't come to any harm."

" What if a swell sets in and we can't push off?" asked the Second cautiously.

" No fear of that," replied the keeper. " We always get four or five hours' notice of that. I haven't seen the glass so high and steady since the end of June."

" Isn't it your dinner-time?"

" Yes, but that don't signify."

" Doesn't it?" rejoined Ned laughingly. " We haven't had ours and we're hungry!"

" Then don't let me keep you, my lad. As my father used to say: 'A plague on the man who comes between me and my victuals!' Tell young Ron from me we're expecting the lot of you here at half past one."

CHAPTER XIV THE LONE BULL LIGHTHOUSE

Ron Bradley would have jumped to the lighthouse keeper's invitation had he been an ordinary member of the crew. He had often wished to see over a lighthouse, and although he had been close to the Lone Bull on several occasions he had never before had the opportunity to do so.

But he wasn't an ordinary member of the crew. He was both Patrol-leader and acting skipper of the *Nut*, and this brought home to him his sense of responsibility. Wouldn't he be pointed out as an inefficient skipper if he went ashore and during his absence the yacht met with disaster — parting with her anchor, for instance?

"There's no reason why you fellows shouldn't go," he suggested, after Ned had given him the keeper's assurance that very little time would be lost, on account of the adverse tide. "I'll stay here and give an eye to things. There are one or two jobs that require attention."

"You cut off and leave those to me, Ron," interjected Mr. Miles. "I'll take charge while you're ashore, and if anything happens that requires your return I'll make good use of the fog-horn! I don't think there will, and in any case it will give Nick the chance of a scamper ashore, even if the shore consists of rocks and seaweed!"

The mention of his dog broke down Ron's objections.

"Thanks awfully, sir! Now, you fellows, what about grub?"

"All ready!" reported George. "Soup, dumplings, spuds, carrots——"

The rest of the description of the menu was drowned by the crew's boisterous shouts of acclamation. They were hungry, and looked to Cookie to satisfy their needs, and he had not disappointed them. The wonder of it was how George, in the strictly limited size of the galley, had contrived to provide a jolly good meal for six hungry people and the dog!

"We'll wash up for you, Cookie!" declared Lofty at the end of the repast.

"No, you won't!" declared George firmly. "A precious mess there'd be with you fellows falling over each other. Out you clear, and I'll be finished in half the time you'd take!"

He was as good as his word, so that ten minutes before the time fixed for the crew to go ashore every utensil had been properly washed, dried and put away in its proper place. George wasn't a badge-hunter, and those he had gained meant continued efficiency. His cook's badge, for example, wasn't meant as a medal for something he had done, but a visible testimony to his present and future skill in that line.

Going ashore presented some difficulty. The dinghy would not carry more than three persons, so it meant three trips with a full complement since Nick required as much space as the others, especially as in his exuberance he was continually jumping from one end of the dinghy to the other.

The moment he leapt ashore he was off, chasing rats that weren't to be found on the rock, and disturbing gulls that were!

" He can't go far, that's certain," remarked Ron. " So we'll leave him to his own devices till it's time to go on board again."

Climbing the vertical ladder, the Sea Scouts found themselves inside the circular tower, where a spiral staircase, giving access to various living-, sleeping- and store-rooms, led to the gallery around the lantern.

" You don't get many visitors, do you?" asked Ned.

The head keeper smiled.

" A few in the summer months. They run motor-boat trips from Dockingham when the sea's calm, which it rarely is. But they make up for their small numbers by the funny questions they ask. Don't they, Bill?"

"Eh, that they do," agreed his assistant. "Remember that gal they said was a film star? Asked where the lift was, and when we said that there wasn't one she stopped at the foot of the ladder out in the rain—and it *was* coming down—until the rest of the party had gone round."

"Yes, and afterwards we saw the film at Otherport, and the way that girl climbed a cliff made me fair giddy," rejoined the head keeper. "And I'm used to heights."

"As likely as not the cliff was horizontal when it was shot," suggested Ned. "Lot of that sort of stuff is a fake."

"No doubt you're right," agreed Bill. "I always said that if she couldn't climb yon ladder she couldn't shin up that cliff."

With justifiable pride the head keeper showed his visitors the lantern and entered into a long explanation of the use of dioptric lenses, the synchronizing mechanism that controlled the "group occulting flashes", and other important factors contributing to the efficiency of the light.

"Not a speck of dust anywhere," remarked Lofty.

"It takes four hours every day to keep the lantern clean," declared their guide. "Which reminds me of another lady visitor we had. 'You must find time hang heavily on your hands in summer-time. The lantern is hardly used; no wonder you can keep it so brightly polished!' And I'd just finished putting in a morning's work on the job! Do you know why there are always three keepers on duty in a lighthouse?"

"It's a three-man job, I suppose," suggested Musty.

"M'yes," agreed the guide dubiously. "But three years ago there used to be only two. Once on the Eddystone—you'll remember a keeper was taken ill some while back and it was days before the Trinity House tender could get him off—well, it was nearly a couple of centuries before that; one of the keepers died and his mate, because he was afraid he'd be accused of murdering him, kept the body in the tower for six weeks before the relief keepers arrived. Ever since then Trinity House made it a rule that there must always be three men in the lighthouse at one time."

"Have you seen many shipwrecks from here?" asked George.

"Not many, thank heaven! That's what the lighthouse is for—to prevent them. But once, I remember well, on a November night—— Hello! That dog of yours is busy!"

Ninety feet below the gallery, and looking no larger than a rat, Nick was facing a greyish animal of three or four times his size.

"What is it?" asked Ron anxiously. "Is it dangerous?"

"It would be," replied the head keeper; "that is, if your dog didn't keep his distance. It's a seal and they're pretty tough customers at close quarters. One of our fellows had his fingers bitten almost through by a seal."

"Here?" asked Lofty.

"No, on the east coast. There, he's off. He's dived into that pool."

"Are there many seals here?" asked George.

"Very few. Strangely enough, it's only of recent years that they've put in an appearance in the English Channel. For some reason they wouldn't go through the Straits of Dover. On the east coast, especially in the Wash, they swarm."

"Do you ever shoot them?" asked Ned.

"Shoot them? Certainly not," declared the keeper. "They do no harm and their skins are valueless. You see, they aren't the seals from which women's coats are made. No, we draw the line at shooting. Any irresponsible fool can take life, and, once taken, no one can give it back. We see quite enough slaughter as it is."

"How's that?" asked Lofty.

"Birds in stormy weather," explained his guide. "At night-time they're attracted by the lantern and dash themselves to death against the glass. I've seen the place where you're standing ankle-deep with dead birds—larks and starlings, but mostly gulls."

"You were telling us what happened one November night," prompted Ron, whose anxiety for his pet had been allayed by the disappearance of the seal.

"Oh yes; it was about one in the morning, wind sou'-sou'-east and blowing gale force, with heavy snow showers. I'd gone outside to clear the frozen snow from the lantern when I caught sight of a topsail schooner—about a couple of hundred tons—driving straight down on us. All she had was a close-reefed staysail that was flogging itself to bits.

"I reckon she was drawing nine feet. See that rock?" He pointed to a jagged pinnacle about twenty yards from the base of the lighthouse. "That's awash at high-water springs and the rise o' tide is only thirteen feet. Well now, on she comes like a train. I could do nothing but hold on, expecting to see the tower come down like a hundred of bricks. I could see people aboard her, but they couldn't do anything either. Her rudder had been carried away, we heard later.

"Then a terrific sea swept her clear. She couldn't have missed us by more than four or five feet, and she passed between the lighthouse and yon rock. If she hadn't been on the top of that wave she would have struck and broken her back in two twos, and none of us here could have lifted as much as a little finger to help them. Ten seconds later, and she was lost to sight."

"Did she sink?" asked Ned.

"No; she drove close in a couple of miles to Deadmen's Bay, where by rights she should have been smashed up on the beach."

The Sea Scout's knew Deadmen's Bay, where many a sailing vessel and more than one steamer have been driven to their doom by on-shore gales.

"Were the crew saved?" asked Ned.

"Yes, and the schooner. She must have had a charmed life that night, for another tremendous sea carried her completely over the beach into the pool beyond. There the crew managed to let go their last remaining anchor and it held. When the tide fell they were as snug as if they were in Otherport Harbour. But the schooner couldn't be got out again, and so her gear was taken out of her and she was sold to some man who turned her into a floating tea-house at Bickerly, that's up at the eastern end of the pool. Hello! That dog of yours in trouble again? We'd better look lively to see what's wrong."

There was a hurried descent of the spiral staircase and down the vertical outside ladder to the rocks. Guided by the yelps of the dog, for he was now hidden by intervening ledges, the two keepers and the Sea Scouts, stumbling over the slippery kelp and floundering through shallow pools, reached the scene of Nick's latest adventure.

The dog had ceased yelping and was attacking with ferocious vigour something that at first sight appeared to be half a dozen strands of a large rope—only, some of the "strands" were writhing and beating the air like whips.

Nick's assailant was a squid—a species of octopus with tentacles six or seven feet in length, although its body was no larger than a football.

At first the fight had gone in the squid's favour. It had wound its tentacles round the dog, but owing to the latter's hairy coat, the suckers had been unable to obtain a hold. Then, once over this initial fright, Nick, although hampered by being in the water, had gone for the squid's body and already the loathsome creature was nearly dead. The pool was discoloured with its watery blood and by a copious discharge of inky fluid, under cover of which it had tried, though ineffectually, to beat a retreat.

"Don't you go too close," warned the head keeper. "If those suckers get hold of your hand they'll tear the skin off. The squid's given your dog best!"

Evidently Nick was of the same opinion, for he broke off the fight and came up to his master, panting yet wagging his stumpy tail. Except for the fact that he had lost a few isolated patches of hair, he seemed to be unhurt.

"They're things to be killed on sight," observed the keeper. "They aren't animals. It's the same with sharks, the seaman's natural enemy, though there was a case near Weymouth a little while since when a fisherman was questioned by the Society for Prevention of Cruelty to Animals for stabbing a shark with his knife! Fair ridiculous, I reckon!"

The Sea Scouts retraced their way to the lighthouse. Already dozens of gulls were hovering over the scene of the encounter, uttering raucous cries as they swooped down for dainty morsels from the mangled squid.

"Well, you've seen all there is to be seen in the lighthouse," observed the keeper. "By the time you're aboard and under way the tide'll be in your favour."

"Really?" asked Ron dubiously. "The east-going tide made at seven this morning and it's now only three o'clock."

"Exactly," rejoined the man. "It just happens that along this part of the coast the tide turns two hours earlier than it does in the offing. I should have thought that you Sea Scouts knew that."

"We didn't," admitted the Patrol-leader frankly.

"Never too late to learn," added the keeper cheerfully. "And I'll tell you another thing.

Wind's nearly sou'west and falling light. About sunset you can expect a steady off-shore breeze—that almost always happens in fine settled weather along the south coast—and you can ride safely at anchor in Dockingham Roads."

The Sea Scouts embarked in relays as before, Ron, Lofty and the dog being the last to leave.

"Thanks awfully for showing us round," said the Patrol-leader.

"And thanks for bringing us our letters and papers," replied the head keeper. "And particularly the 'bacca. My mates and I were down to the last ounce! You've done a right Good Turn!"

CHAPTER XV

"ABANDON SHIP!"

Instead of folding the collapsible dinghy and stowing it on deck, where it took up a lot of much-needed room, Ron decided to tow the little tender, since with the wind in its present quarter it would cause only a little drag upon the yacht.

"Up mainsail, lads!" ordered the Patrol-leader briskly. "Heave short the cable!"

The mainsail, thanks to the well-greased track, was set without a hitch; but when Lofty and George attempted to break out and weigh the anchor, they found that in spite of their united efforts they were unable to get it off the ground.

"We're foul of something, Skipper!" announced Lofty breathlessly.

Ron was not greatly surprised. Anchoring on a rocky bottom always entailed that risk.

"It's a jolly good thing we buoyed the anchor," he declared. "I'll go out in the dinghy and pick up the buoy."

This he did, bringing the buoy and its end of the rope back on the fore-deck.

Under normal conditions it should have been an easy matter to free the anchor. By pulling on the buoy rope, the lower end of which was bent to the crown of the anchor, it ought to have been possible to lift the palm clear of whatever it had fouled—probably a crevice in a rock.

But this time it didn't work. Although Ron and Lofty heaved away until they were afraid that the strain would part the rope, the anchor stubbornly refused to budge.

Then they tried paying out more cable and attempting to break out the anchor by putting the yacht ahead under power. That also failed, not once but many times. Unless the *Nut* was to remain there indefinitely, the only thing that remained to be done was to cut the cable just above the water-level, buoy it and hope for the best! That wasn't a pleasant thought. For one thing, the anchor wasn't theirs; for another, all they would have left with which to buoy up was a small kedge, that could not be relied upon to hold the yacht.

Baffled, the Patrol-leader did the best thing: he asked Mr. Miles for his advice.

" I think I know what's happened," said the Group S.M. " The buoy rope must have taken a turn or two round the cable; so that instead of raising the anchor by the crown you're putting a strain on the stock. Now heave taut on the cable. We can't see where the turns are and in what way they run, so we must adopt the 'trial and error' method. Pass the buoy and the rope under the cable clockwise and then heave on the rope."

This they tried again without success.

"Couldn't I dive and free it, sir?" suggested Lofty.

"You might, but you are not going to," replied Mr. Miles. "I'm not doubting your ability, but there are such things as getting foul of a rope, and then we could do nothing to save you from a sticky end! Now, have another try, Ron! Take two turns in the opposite direction."

Again the effort failed to achieve expectations.

"Now three turns clockwise," suggested the G.S.M. "You see, we are alternately progressing in both directions until the turns are taken out. We've already proved there are more than one."

Anxiously the crew watched the next stage of the proceedings, Mr. Miles especially so. He knew that if the rope were foul of the anchor stock the method would fail, and he was banking upon the possibility of the double round turn occurring between the stock and the waterline.

Another powerful heave and Ron and Lofty sat down somewhat painfully—the P.L. on the bitts and his chum with the small of his back against a belaying pin in the spider band.

Not that they minded! The much-desired result had been attained. The anchor was clear of the sea bed.

Quickly the stubborn " hook " was brought inboard and stowed. The roller foresail was broken out and the helm put up. Barely heeling to the now gentle breeze, the *Nut* gathered way and headed shorewards before passing through the wide but shallow channel that separated the Lone Bull Rock from the mainland.

Here they certainly carried the tide, as they had been informed, but the breeze dropped to a proper " Paddy's hurricane ". The surface of the sea was like a sheet of glass, while the heat of the sun, that was still well above the horizon, not only made itself directly felt, but was augmented by the reflected glare.

For more than an hour the *Nut* drifted, boxing the compass again and again, yet not carrying any way. The tiller swung idly; the slack of the mainsheets was frequently trailing in the water. In vain the Sea Scouts adhered to certain traditions of the sea, whistling for a breeze and scratching the mast. Even the latter supposedly infallible method of bringing a favourable wind failed.

Yet Ron stubbornly adhered to his determination not to make use of the motor. His chums, even though they were Scouts, failed to smile under these circumstances and chafed under the prolonged spell of inaction.

It was not until the sun was on the point of sinking that the Patrol-leader reluctantly told Musty to get busy with the engine. In an hour or so the adverse tide would start and Dockingham Roads were still a dozen miles away. The Lone Bull Lighthouse was only a few miles astern, its slender shaft standing out sharply against the western sky.

Lifting a section of the cockpit floor, Musty adjusted the controls and gave the starting handle a swing. Except for a slight hissing sound, nothing happened. He tried again and again.

Then he looked up, perspiration streaming down his face.

"It's funny, Skipper!" he declared. "There's something wrong somewhere."

"What is it?" asked Ron.

"Dunno; she was running all right when we tried breaking out the anchor. There's no reason why she shouldn't run now, as far as I can make out."

Resuming his ostrich-like posture, Musty tried the motor again, to a running fire of advice from his chums.

"Are you doing the job or am I?" he asked.

"Keep your hair on, old son!" exclaimed Lofty.

" You have a shot at the confounded thing, then!" rejoined Musty, as he wiped his face for the third time in as many minutes.

Lofty swung the starting handle until he, too, was running with perspiration and the palm of his right hand sore with grasping the brass grip.

" Ain't she a pig!" he ejaculated. " My hand's raw."

" Then put some petrol on it," suggested Ned. " That's a good cure for chafed hands. Tickle the carburettor and let some of the juice overflow."

Lofty did as the Second had suggested, holding his hand palm uppermost for the air to evaporate the volatile fluid.

He waited a minute or so, and then turned to Musty.

" Look here, Musty," he announced. " This isn't petrol; it's water!"

It certainly was. The beads of moisture confirmed the Sea Scout's statement.

Again Musty went down on his knees and bent over the engine. Sure enough, the carburettor was flooding, but most of the overflow consisted of water.

" Gasket's gone, lads!" he declared laconically.

" Sure?" asked Ron anxiously, for now that the motor was out of action he was wishing that it was running! " I can't see how water gets into a carburettor even if the gasket's gone."

"Well, it has," replied Musty. "The cooling water has leaked through to the cylinders and from there through the induction pipe to the carburettor. It'll mean taking off the cylinder heads and fitting a new gasket."

"How long will that take?"

"An hour, perhaps two," answered Musty; "but I'll be as sharp as I can."

It did not take long to remove the cylinder head. A gap in the fibre gasket confirmed the amateur mechanic's diagnosis.

"And there's not a spare one on board," he announced. "I'll have to make one out of brown paper. Slice open that bag for me, will you, Musty?"

It was a long and tricky task. Three times Musty carefully cut sheets of brown paper to shape and oiled them before trying to fit them, and three times the makeshift gaskets broke before the cylinder head could be replaced.

To complicate matters, it was growing dark, and since an ordinary lantern was too risky to use owing to the petrol fumes, the work had to be resumed by the aid of an electric torch.

"Try cutting the outside edge when the cylinder head's firmly bolted down," advised Mr. Miles.

That did the trick, and at a quarter to eleven—the prophesied off-shore breeze not making itself felt—the engine was restarted and a course shaped against a two-knot ebb for the roadstead that held the promise of a quiet night's anchorage.

The *Nut*, since she was not under sail, was displaying the customary navigation lights—red and green to port and starboard respectively, and a white light on her mast at a height of seven feet above the deck.

Most of the crew were below, leaving Ron at the helm and George keeping him company, when the latter exclaimed: " There's a vessel coming up astern of us, Skipper!"

The Patrol-leader threw a brief glance astern. There was nothing much for him to do but to hold his course, since the other craft was the overtaking vessel. Then it occurred to him that she might not be able to see the *Nut's* navigation lights.

" Give a flash with your torch, George!" suggested Ron. " That'll draw their attention."

As a result, the other craft altered her course slightly to starboard, and then George pointed out that there was another vessel under power that had up to now been following in her wake.

Again the warning light was shown and the second of the overtaking vessels went a little to port, which meant that the *Nut* would be somewhere between them as they drew ahead.

This they began to do, since both were considerably faster than the auxiliary-engined yacht; but when abreast they slowed down.

"What craft is that?" hailed a gruff voice.

"Yacht *Nut*!" replied Ron.

There was a pause during which the craft on the *Nut's* starboard side—she proved to be a motor launch of about forty feet in length—edged closer.

"My orders are to put your crew ashore and take your yacht in tow to Dockingham! You've five minutes to collect your traps!"

The Patrol-leader was too taken aback to reply to this astonishing and unexpected demand.

He opened the cabin doors. In the saloon the three Sea Scouts off duty were sleeping peacefully. Mr. Miles was behind closed doors in the fore-cabin.

"Mr. Miles!" exclaimed Ron anxiously.

The G.S.M. appeared almost at once. Ron guessed rightly that he already had an inkling of what was transpiring and was only waiting to be called before shouldering responsibility.

Coming out from the brightly illuminated cabin into the darkness, Mr. Miles had to wait until his eyes grew accustomed to the night.

"D'ye want me to tell you again?" demanded the raucous voice from the motor launch. "We're landing you boys and taking the yacht in tow to Dockingham. Them's my orders and you'll jolly well have to carry them out!"

" Who's orders, did you say?" inquired Mr. Miles.

There was another pause, during which the crew of the motor launch could be heard conferring in undertones.

" Owner's orders!" came the delayed reply, for the skipper of the launch had not expected to find a man on board the yacht—only the five Sea Scouts who had taken the *Nut* out of Otherport Harbour.

" Really! What is your owner's name?" asked the Group Scoutmaster.

" Mr. Gunville—Mr. Tarrant Gunville."

" How interesting! We thought he was in hospital."

" So he is! That didn't stop him from sending us a wire asking us to take charge of his yacht. It's going to blow hard and that made him anxious to get the yacht into the harbour."

" And you can produce the telegram?"

There was another subdued conversation. Mr. Miles's presence had rather upset things. It didn't look as if he'd be convinced by this plausible story.

" Come on, sir!" continued the man persuasively. " We can't hang about all night. Time's precious. Stand by to pass us your warp."

" We'll do nothing of the sort!"

The skipper of the launch altered his tone.

" We've got to carry out our owner's orders. If you won't heave us a line we'll come alongside!"

" I wouldn't, if I were you," rejoined Mr. Miles. " You'll be held responsible for any damage done. Lofty, call up the harbour-master at Dockingham. Ask him to send a police launch to our assistance, and say we're held up by a gang in a couple of motor-boats!"

Lofty " tumbled to it ".

Although the *Nut* carried no wireless—not even a receiving set—he played up to the G.S.M.'s bluff.

It was the work of a few seconds to bring a spare six-volt battery to the foot of the accommodation ladder. With one end of a length of insulated wire made fast to the negative terminal and the other tapping the positive one, the resulting series of crackles as the battery " shorted " gave a convincing imitation of a low-powered transmitter in action.

Lofty began by calling up Dockingham, making Morse signals in case the fellows in the motor launch were able to read the succession of dots and dashes.

" Call acknowledged, sir!" he reported.

" Carry on with the message!" rejoined Mr. Miles.

Lofty did so, almost running the battery down in the process.

All the while the crew of the motor launch were inactive and silent, except for whispered misgivings. Without a doubt they were greatly perturbed at the thought that the *Nut* was sending out a call for assistance.

Mr. Miles considered that the moment had arrived to carry the war into the enemy's camp.

" I thought you were coming alongside!" he exclaimed. " We'd like to have a closer look at you! Unless I'm much mistaken I saw two of you at Otherport yesterday; and didn't one of you say something about ' getting the stuff off her '? Yes, I'm certain I'll know you again!"

This was too much for the crew of the launch. Without replying, her skipper gave the engine full throttle. She shot ahead and was soon lost to sight.

Apparently the second boat had followed her example. At any rate, she had put out her navigation lights and was now no longer to be seen.

" What was Mr. Gunville's idea, sir?" asked Ned.

" Mr. Gunville had nothing to do with it," replied Mr. Miles. " It was a frame-up that didn't come off!"

" What was the idea, sir?" asked Ron.

" What exactly it is, I can't say," replied the G.S.M. " For some reason—and what that is, I don't know—there's a gang who seem to have a grudge against Mr. Gunville. Quite possibly it was a couple of these fellows who knocked him insensible; but what puzzles me, as it does the Otherport police, is his strong disinclination to assist the constabulary. They feel certain that he was sandbagged in the alley where they found a pool of blood, while he persists in asserting he was felled as soon as he stepped ashore."

" Don't you think, sir——" began Ned.

" That it's time you turned in again," interrupted Mr. Miles. " Ron and I will remain on deck until we arrive off Dockingham; and then, if you're wanted, we'll give you a shout. Now, no yarning! Down below you go!"

Leaving Ron at the helm—for by this time the harbour lights were visible and consequently no compass course was necessary—the G.S.M. settled himself in the cockpit and puffed reflectively at his pipe.

Undoubtedly, he thought, it was a good thing he had been on board to handle the situation. Goodness knows what might have happened if there had been only the five lads on board. They might have accepted the rogues' statement and allowed themselves to be set ashore; and then what would have happened to the yacht? Possibly the crew of the launch might have scuttled her. It was hardly likely that they would take her into Dockingham. And what was the " stuff " they were so keen on " getting out of her "? Hardly part of her ordinary equipment, but if not that, what? Certainly nothing of a contraband nature, otherwise Customs Official Badger would have discovered it. And yet——

Mr. Miles gave it up. He wasn't a detective. If there were anything that brought the *Nut* under official suspicion, that would be the job of the Customs to deal with. His task was to exercise a more or less normal supervision over the Seagulls until the *Nut* was safely handed over to Tarrant Gunville's agent at Easthaven.

" You know how to switch off the engine, Ron?" he asked.

" Yes, sir!"

" Then we won't disturb the others. If we can pick up a mooring so much the better; if not, we'll anchor. I'm keeping anchor-watch for the rest of the night."

" Will those fellows show up again?" asked the Patrol-leader.

" I don't think so. All the same, it's well to Be Prepared. We're going to lie in an open roadstead and, even with the best precautions, a yacht is liable to drag. Now I'll take her for a spell. You'd better go below and get some grub so that you won't turn in supperless."

By the time Ron had finished a hasty though satisfying meal, the *Nut* was abreast the entrance to the harbour. It was not Mr. Miles's intention to take her into the somewhat crowded port; since the weather looked like continuing fair, it was better to bring up outside and so save the customary harbour dues.

Broad on the port beam was the green light on the east pier; ahead and beyond the fairway a line of twinkling white lights indicated the mooring-ground for yachts.

" All ready to let go, Ron?" asked the helmsman.

" Yes, sir; anchor's buoyed."

" We'll try for a vacant mooring. Got your torch handy? You'll need it to pick up the buoy."

Armed with the torch, Ron went for'ard and, steadying himself by the forestay, swept the surface with the powerful spot-light.

" Starboard a bit, sir!" he sang out as the ray picked up a small, white-painted cask about fifty yards off. " Stop the engine! She'll just do it."

With the propeller in neutral and breasting the slight flood tide, the *Nut* ran gently up to the mooring.

" Got it!" exclaimed the P.L. as with a well-judged effort he secured the buoy with the boathook and brought it inwards. The buoy rope followed, and the chain bridle, which Ron made fast round the bitts.

Then the engine was switched off and the navigation lamps extinguished. The riding-light was hoisted on the forestay and the *Nut* was properly moored for the rest of the night.

" Tired?" asked Mr. Miles.

" Rather, sir!"

" All right! Turn in as soon as you like."

" Good night, sir! I say, there's a motor boat coming towards us!"

" Not unusual in a recognized anchorage," rejoined the G.S.M. " Someone putting off to one of those yachts."

Mr. Miles was adrift in his surmise. The launch ran alongside the *Nut* and a voice gave the all too familiar hail: " Yacht ahoy! What's your name? Where are you from?"

With feelings of relief Ron realized that the voice was not that of the mysterious fellow who had tried to induce the Seagulls to abandon the *Nut*.

It was the Customs launch from Dockingham.

"*Nut*, eh? From Otherport? Sorry, but we'll have to come aboard and look round."

"But we haven't arrived from a foreign port," protested Mr. Miles.

"I don't say you have, sir; but all the same we've our duty to do."

"At this hour of night? There are four lads—Sea Scouts—asleep below. Is it necessary to disturb them? The yacht has already been examined by the Otherport Customs Officers."

"We know that, sir!" replied the man, with a short laugh. "Well, if you promise you won't slip your moorings we'll be alongside at eight in the morning. No one's been ashore here, yet?"

"No, we've only just arrived."

The officer flashed his torch along the yacht's deck and then astern of her.

"Then where's your dinghy?" he asked suspiciously.

The canvas cockleshell that had been towing astern was no longer there. One end of the painter was still bent to the cleat, but its rope had been cut through by some sharp instrument, leaving about twelve feet of it trailing in the water.

"It must have been that motor launch!" declared Ron.

"What motor launch?" snapped the Customs man.

" I think I'd better explain," interposed Mr. Miles. " About an hour and a half ago, when we were roughly six miles west of Dockingham, two motor boats closed with us. The crew of one of them informed us that Mr. Gunville—that's the owner of the yacht—had given orders to them to tow us into Dockingham. I challenged the truth of their assertion and after a bit they sheered off."

The Customs officer turned to one of the boatmen.

" Any motor boat left here to-night, Jackson?"

" No, sir; not to my knowledge."

" H'm! You didn't see them cut your dinghy's painter?"

" No."

" Painter may have been rotten and parted by itself."

" It was almost a new rope," declared Ron.

" You'd better report it to the Receiver of Wrecks to-morrow, sir," suggested the Customs Officer. " I'll wish you good night, and " —he added significantly—" I'll see you at eight o'clock!"

In spite of the excitement and late hours the crew of the *Nut* were up, merry and bright, at seven o'clock, to find that there was a steady westerly breeze and a cloud-flecked sky. The tide, too, was in their favour. There were half a dozen reasons why they should get under way, particularly the fact that the favouring breeze was running to waste as far as they were concerned; but there was one reason why they should remain—to await the promised visit of the Water Guard Officer of Her Majesty's Board of Customs and Excise, to give that worthy his official title.

However, after the Sea Scouts had had breakfast and had stowed everything away—they were determined that the boarding officer would find the yacht shipshape alow and aloft—the Customs launch was sighted as it cleared the harbour entrance.

" She has our dinghy in tow, sir!" declared Ron.

" If it isn't ours it's her exact image," added Ned.

The launch ran alongside and made fast. In her were two boatmen who had not been in her on her previous visit, and their previous acquaintance, the Customs officer.

" Mornin'!" he greeted the *Nut's* crew. " We've brought back your dinghy. She's a bit the worse for wear."

It certainly was. The inner lining—she was of the double-skin collapsible type—had been ripped by some sharp implement along almost its entire length under both gunwales.

" How did that happen?" inquired Mr. Miles. " It hasn't been done accidentally."

" Far from it," agreed the Water Guard

officer. " Someone's been looking for something."

" So it would seem. But what was the object? As far as we know, there was—and is—nothing of value on board, other than the yacht's ordinary gear and equipment."

" And I'm not so sure about that," declared the officer significantly. " That's why I told you I was going to rummage round. Mind you, I'm not suggesting you're concerned. Quite possibly the owner—Mr. Gunville, I think you said?—knows nothing about it. On the other hand, he may."

" But you haven't told us how and where you found the dinghy," Mr. Miles reminded him.

" A local fishing-smack picked her up and brought her in early this morning, soon after sunrise, and handed her over to us. You see, we've rove a new painter for you; the old one was cut off short at the stem-head. But that's not the end of the story. We'd hardly taken her over when a Dockingham motor passenger launch owner reported that two of his boats were missing. He'd left them, safely moored, alongside his landing-stage overnight — that was at eleven o'clock—and at six o'clock when his men went down to get them ready for the day's work they were nowhere to be seen. About half an hour later one of our men on duty at Fisherton Gap reported by telephone that there were two large motor launches left high and dry, and unattended, on the beach. So I got in touch with the County police, and they've just informed us that a large open tourer car, with eight men packed into her, stopped for petrol at Nixworth. The garage man hadn't taken the number of the car; but one answering that description with a crowd in her ought to be fairly conspicuous."

" Even now I don't see the object of these gentlemen's unwanted attentions," observed Mr. Miles. " The two I noticed at Otherport seemed intent upon ' lifting ' something from this yacht and actually made the attempt, though it was frustrated, mainly by this dog here. I made a point of warning Water Guard Officer Badger at Otherport, and although he took action he was a few minutes too late."

" Well, they've had something of a scare, that's evident," added the officer. " I don't suppose they'll trouble you again. So, since you must be anxious to be getting under way, I'll push on with my job as quickly as possible."

With that he produced the tools of his trade, which resembled those used by the efficient Mr. Badger when he " rummaged " the yacht on her arrival at Otherport.

In order to save time, Ron and Ned pointed out to him the various parts of the yacht that Mr. Badger had probed and examined without result. The Customs officer was not to be diverted from his purpose. Again the floor-boards were taken up, the cabin panelling removed, bulkhead tested for double space. Even the sacks of provisions given to the crew just before they left Otherport were examined.

"You've had your sails up?" asked the searcher-in-chief.

"Yes, sir," replied Ron.

"H'm! I'm afraid there's only one thing to be done: to wish you 'au revoir and a pleasant voyage!'"

"I'm glad there is, sir!" rejoined the Patrol-leader.

"We'll put it that way, then," amended the Customs officer. "'Afraid' is hardly the word to use; but from my point of view it expresses my disappointment on drawing blank!"

The launch cast off and headed towards the harbour, leaving the crew of the *Nut* to set the disordered saloon and fore-cabin to rights.

"I wonder if Mr. Gunville has insured the yacht," said Lofty. "If so, he'll be able to recover the cost of the repairs to the dinghy."

"He might," rejoined Ned. "But isn't there something about acts committed by the King's enemies and piracy being exceptions? I reckon the insurance people would be right in declaring that those fellows who tried to board us last night were pirates."

The argument was warmly debated until

Ron interrupted the proceedings by ordering the foresail to be unrolled and the moorings dropped.

Not until the yacht was under way with headsail only did he order the mainsail to be hoisted. Then, with the mainsheet well slacked off, the *Nut* ran before the breeze on the last stage of her voyage to Easthaven.

"Isn't this topping!" exclaimed Ned. "Sailing beats motor-boating any day!"

"Does it?" rejoined Lofty. "How about a flat calm?"

It was nearly midday. The *Nut* was about five miles off the land. The wind had veered slightly and was blowing diagonally off shore, so that the yacht was sailing free, though without the risk of an accidental gybe as might have happened had the breeze been dead aft.

In consequence it was quite safe for some of the crew, wearing shorts only, to sprawl on the cabin top, without the chance of being hurled overboard by a devastating sweep of the boom—a not infrequent cause of fatalities resulting from a gybe.

Ned was at the helm, Ron in the cockpit and engaged in whipping a rope's end. George was engaged upon what was a congenial task as far as he was concerned, namely, preparing dinner in the galley.

Mr. Miles had made himself scarce from the time the *Nut* got under way. Now that the interview with the Customs was over he was able to hand back the command of the yacht to the Patrol-leader. Having arrears of sleep to make up, he had retired to the fore-cabin in the knowledge that, should the necessity arise, he would be warned by the crew.

The *Nut* was not alone. She was close to one of the principal steamship tracks of the English Channel where vessels converge to the west'ard of Dungeness before making for the Downs.

At the moment there were two liners, three tramps, an oil-tanker and a couple of Thames barges within sight.

"It's strange how they seem to bunch together," remarked Ned. "We had the sea to ourselves half an hour ago and we may again before we sight Easthaven. There's one thing, we're well inside that lot. They won't have to alter course for us!"

"That collier's taking it green!" exclaimed Lofty. "Look how she's putting her nose under!"

"Yes, 'gainst wind and tide," added Ron, glancing up from his work. "And we aren't even taking a drop of spray on board. How's the grub getting on, George?"

"You'll be eating your dinner twenty minutes from now!" replied the cook confidently. "Twelve o'clock sharp!"

The stream of shipping thinned. The nearer craft, a Thames barge on a parallel course to the *Nut*, was about a mile off; but right ahead was a cargo vessel on a westerly course.

The *Nut* was doing about four knots, the tramp about nine, consequently the distance between them rapidly decreased.

According to the *Rule of the Road at Sea*, the steamer should give way to the sailing craft. She made no immediate effort to do so. Probably her quartermaster at the wheel considered the *Nut* too insignificant.

"Hadn't I better put the helm up?" asked Ned.

"We've the right of way," replied Ron, "but we'd better edge to starboard a bit. Ever heard the rhyme about Andrew Jay?"

"The motorist who died defending his right of way?"

"Yes; well, how's this?

"Here lies the wreck of the yacht *Blue Jay*;
She was sunk defending her right of way.
She was right—close-hauled on the starboard tack,
But that didn't prevent her getting a crack."

"'From the bows of a blundering fishing smack!'" added Lofty, raising his head to take a better look at the oncoming vessel. "She's altering helm, so it's all right."

The change of direction enabled the Seagulls to obtain a three-quarter length view of the steamship. She was a Swedish ship, as was evident by her ensign—a yellow cross on a blue field. Both the fore and aft well-decks were piled high with timber, so that it would be possible to walk from the lower bridge either to the fore-deck or the poop without having to descend or climb a ladder.

" I reckon she'd lose that lot in a gale," opined Lofty. " Do you remember last winter when the beach at Otherport was strewn with wood washed off—— Look, Ron! There's a man overboard!"

The Patrol-leader dropped what he was doing and sprang to his feet.

Less than a cable's length separated the *Nut* from the steamship and they had hardly drawn abeam of each other. The Swede was throwing up a fair amount of spray and rather a heavy bow wave.

" Overboard—where?" asked the Patrol-leader.

" There he is—just clear of her quarter. He's swimming away from her."

" Yes, I see him!" exclaimed Ron.

At first glance there seemed nothing extraordinary in the fact that the man " in the ditch " was striking out away from the craft from which he had fallen. It was advisable to do so to avoid being caught by the suction of the propeller and cut to pieces by the rapidly revolving blades; but when the man continued to swim, instead of conserving his strength by treading water until he could be picked up, the Patrol-leader came to the correct conclusion that he had deliberately jumped overboard in the hope of being rescued by the yacht.

He was in fact swimming strongly in an effort to bring himself ahead of the *Nut's* bows.

Nobody on board the timber ship seemed to have noticed the incident; and when Lofty hailed her with the warning cry of " Man overboard ", an officer on the bridge merely waved his arm as if in acknowledgment of a friendly greeting.

Ron had his own problem to work out.

Owing to the speed at which the *Nut* was going through the water and to the fact that there would not be time to reduce sail, they would not stand a chance of picking the man up. He would probably be knocked senseless by the yacht's forefoot.

" Stand by the foresail sheets!" ordered the Patrol-leader. " Everybody aft! Down helm, Ned; at that! Ready to go about!"

Ned " tumbled to it ". He was to steer the *Nut* well clear of the swimmer and then come round head to wind so as to get way off her.

Twenty yards to lee'ard of the swimmer, Ron gave the word: " Lee-ho! Down helm! Haul in the mainsheet!"

Round spun the handy little yacht like a top. Then, with the foresail now a-weather, she crept slowly towards the swimmer, so that a couple of strokes brought her alongside.

Without any fuss the man swam towards the now almost stationary yacht, where Lofty and the Patrol-leader assisted him into the cockpit.

Meanwhile the steamer had reversed her engines. Her crew were preparing to lower a boat, to the obvious concern of the rescued swimmer. Then she forged ahead again, since her captain was assured of the man's safety, and resumed her former course.

The Sea Scouts were now able to take stock of the foreigner they had pulled " out of the ditch ". He could hardly be termed a man. They judged his age to be about sixteen. He was full-featured, with dark, almost black, hair. He was wearing only a ragged vest and trousers. In spite of the roundness of his face and the depth of his chest, his arms and legs were abnormally thin, while the ribs under his saturated vest stood out like wooden hoops round a barrel.

As soon as the youth felt assured that the cargo-vessel was not sending a boat for him he cheered up considerably.

" He's a German, I think!" exclaimed Ned, holding out his left hand, which the young foreigner grasped.

" Yes; but how does he know what we are?" asked George. " In what we're wearing now we might be anything!"

" Our Red Ensign, of course!" declared

G 715

"There he is!"

Page 172

Lofty, glancing aloft to where the Red Duster at the peak fluttered in the haze.

The rescued swimmer looked up too and grinned delightedly. Then he burst into a torrent of words, the only ones intelligible to the crew being " Ost Deutschland " and " Stettin ".

" He's from an east-German port," declared Ron.

" Well, what was a German doing on board a Swedish ship?" asked Ned. " And why did he jump overboard?"

" Goodness knows!" replied the Patrol-leader. " Get him some grub, George. He looks hungry! And you might tell Mr. Miles what's up."

" He's asleep," declared George.

" Then wake him," continued Ron. " We have a very good excuse."

Presently the G.S.M. appeared on deck. The German lad sprang to his feet, brought his bare heels together and gave a smart salute. Then, as the *Nut* rolled, he almost lost his balance and had to grasp Ned's arm to prevent himself being flung against the lee coaming.

" How did he get aboard?" asked Mr. Miles.

Ron pointed to the steamship, now a good two miles away and almost hidden by the smoke from the funnel.

"He jumped overboard and swam to us, sir!" he explained. "And he's come to us for help. His name's Jakob, I think."

"So I see," rejoined the G.S.M. "And that complicates matters for us."

"Complicates, sir?"

"Yes, unfortunately. I think I see what's happened. He's a German refugee from Soviet-occupied territory; but it's a bit of a mystery to me why he should have boarded a Swedish ship—that is, if he meant to make his way to England—instead of by means of the Berlin corridor. But the awkward part of the business is, lads, that, although we can't help it, we are assisting in the illegal entry of an alien into the country. I don't suppose for a moment that he has a passport."

"What will happen to him, sir?" asked Lofty.

"We'll have to hand him over to the Immigration Officer at Easthaven, who probably will be one of our attentive friends the Customs! Then he'll be brought before a magistrate, who will order him to be deported."

"Sent back to where he came from, sir?"

"Yes. It seems drastic; but there you are! There must be a limit to the influx of aliens, and those who try to smuggle themselves in are liable to be severely dealt with."

"But he's not a fugitive from justice, sir!"

exclaimed Ned. "Can't we—sort of—adopt him?"

"He's an alien, without permission to land, and, as such, is an undesirable alien, and that's all there is to it! We'll have to see what happens."

"It's jolly hard lines on him, sir," declared Ron. "He looks as if he's been through a lot."

The young refugee, ignorant of his possible fate, was hungrily devouring a hunch of bread and cheese. Quite possibly he had pinned his hopes upon the fact that the *Nut* was flying the Red Ensign, and that, since she was English, he would be safe under the British flag.

"What's your name?" asked Ron.

The boy shook his head.

"I'm Ron!" declared the Patrol-leader, pointing to his chest. "This is Ned—Ned, see? This is George. You; what's your name? It is Jakob, isn't it?"

"Jakob," confirmed the youth. "Jakob!"

He added his surname, but, as far as the crew of the *Nut* were concerned, they got no further with it. George afterwards remarked that it sounded like a cross between an influenza sneeze and a crooner!

Having made a good inroad into the yacht's food stores, Jakob was given a blanket and soon he was sleeping soundly on the cabin floor. It was his own choice of a bunk, and probably was very uncomfortable, but decidedly superior to the numerous and varied " shake-downs " he had experienced on his long trek across part of Eastern Germany.

" Aren't we having any dinner to-day?" asked Musty plaintively. " Didn't you say it would be ready by twelve?"

" It was," declared the cook. " Look at the time now!"

It was ten minutes past one.

CHAPTER XVIII AGROUND

"You carry on with your grub, Lofty!" decided Ron. "I'll take her until you've had it."

"But it's my trick at the helm," expostulated Lofty. "I can wait for dinner just as well as you."

"All the same, my lad," continued the Patrol-leader, "I'm taking over, so off you go, and don't hurry!"

Lofty went with a good grace. He *was* hungry, but he would have continued at the helm quite willingly. Now that he had made a more or less sincere protest he could leave Ron to it with an easy conscience.

Ron, too, was feeling peckish, but he hadn't sent Lofty to his dinner for reasons of consideration towards his hungrier chum.

The wind had fallen light and almost imperceptibly a thin haze had spread over the surface of the sea. Somewhere away on the port bow were the Slimers, an expanse of flat sand covered at quarter flood and extending quite two miles from the shore. Their outer edge was marked by a black-and-white chequered can buoy. Once abreast of the buoy, there are no more outlying dangers to beset the mariner until three miles beyond Easthaven.

It was the presence of haze that might later develop into fog that had decided Ron to take the helm. He had already laid off his course on the chart and had checked his calculations. Having made allowances for the set of the tide and for leeway, he had arrived at the conclusion that a compass course of east-by-south-or-half-south would take the *Nut* well to the south'ard of the Slimers Buoy. His most sanguine estimate was that he wouldn't be off the extremity of the sands in less than a couple of hours.

Presently the mist increased in density. Although the sun was shining upon the upper part of the mainsail and casting an ill-defined shadow upon the cabin-top, it was impossible to see more than a hundred yards ahead.

The fact that the sun was casting shadows eased Ron's task considerably. Instead of having to pay close attention to the compass —always a strain upon nerve and eyesight— he could steer for a minute or so at a time by keeping the shadow of the after starboard shroud in line with the for'ard corner of the skylight. Of course this could not be carried out for any great length of time, since the sun's apparent movement amounts to fifteen degrees every hour; but provided the compass is consulted frequently and the shadow bearing adjusted accordingly, a vessel's course can be held without much difficulty.

Every now and again the Patrol-leader glanced down into the saloon. The other fellows were still tucking in, but judging by the rising volume of talk they were nearing the end of the feed. Either they had awakened Jakob or the smell of the hot grub had overcome his slumbers, for he was sitting up at the table and eating with avidity. Evidently the enormous hunk of bread and a generous slice of cheese had been a mere preliminary, as far as he was concerned!

The mist developed into a fairly heavy fog. With it the wind died away, leaving the *Nut* rolling sluggishly in the long gentle swell, with the visible horizon an ill-defined blur a bare forty feet from where the helmsman sat.

" Sling me out my oilskin, Ned!" called out Ron.

" Right-o!" replied his chum. " I'll come out and give you a spell."

" I'm all right," demurred the Patrol-leader. " The mist's a bit damp. There's no reason why any of you should get soaked."

Ned handed his chum the oilskin. Abandoning the now useless tiller for a few moments, the Patrol-leader struggled into the clammy overcoat.

"Do you mind making a cast before you go below?" asked Ron.

Picking up the coiled lead-line that was lying under the stern bench, Ned took a sounding.

"Mark five, gravelly bottom, Captain!" he reported.

"Good enough!" rejoined Ron, although that information did not convey much beyond the fact that the yacht had twenty-eight feet of water under her keel. The soundings west of the Slimers are almost uniform, the sands being steep-to on the western edge, and since the bottom consists almost everywhere of fine gravel the specimen found in the "arming" of the lead didn't give much help in determining the *Nut's* position.

Still, Ron decided, there was nothing to worry about. The *Nut's* present course, even though her speed was barely one knot, would take her well clear of the Slimers Buoy.

Ned went back to the cabin, to return almost at once with his oilskins on.

"Look here, Ron, I'm taking over, see!" he exclaimed. "You cut off and get your grub. George has put it on the stove to keep hot, but it'll be done to a frizzle if it stops there much longer!"

The Patrol-leader capitulated. He was hungry—ravenously so—and the yacht was in plenty of water.

"Thanks!" he replied. "Course sou' by east and half south. I won't be longer than I can help."

"Don't hurry yourself, old son!" rejoined Ned. "I'll be quite happy."

Ron went into the saloon. Most of the crew were dozing on the settees. Lofty was showing Jakob the pictures in a weekly paper. Mr. Miles, as was often the case, was writing in the fore-cabin.

"Gosh! This is good!" exclaimed the Patrol-leader, as George put a steaming bowl in front of him. "Jolly thoughtful of you. Fancy being able to enjoy hot stew in August."

"Then get outside it!" rejoined the cook, practically though inelegantly. "Yell out when you're ready for the apple tart. I may not be able to hear you with the stove roaring unless you shout!"

But Ron never tasted the apple tart. He had barely completed his first course, which would have satisfied and perhaps finished a good many people, when the yacht shook as her keel hit something with a heavy thud.

Then came a second and a third, though with diminishing violence.

There was a concerted rush on deck. Ned, having abandoned the useless tiller, was trying to fend off the dinghy, which was bumping against the *Nut's* quarter.

"We're aground, Ron!" he exclaimed, stating an obvious though disconcerting fact.

"Get that mainsail down, you fellows!" ordered the Patrol-leader. "Stock the kedge. We'll have to run it out smartly if we are to get off."

The kedge anchor was put into the dinghy and dropped at the full extent of its warp, a good twenty fathoms, astern of the yacht.

"There's hardly any water here!" shouted Musty from the dinghy.

"Come back, then!" ordered Ron, anxious in case the canvas cockleshell might be lost in the fog.

As soon as the dinghy's hands came on board, Ron made the crew stand on the port side in order to increase the yacht's list with a view to reducing her draught. Then a strain was taken on the kedge rope, while others of the crew thrust the looms of the two long sweeps against the sand.

"She's moving!" exclaimed Ned triumphantly. "Keep her going!"

Ron and Ned hauled their hardest on the kedge warp.

"Yes, she's moving!" declared the Patrol-leader.

Fathom after fathom of grass rope came inboard, slowly at first and then with increasing speed, until the cockpit floor was piled high with the coils. Then the kedge itself appeared, dangling over the edge of the counter.

" Keep her going!" admonished Ron, as the two Sea Scouts at the sweeps desisted.

" She hasn't budged a foot, Cap'n!" declared Musty.

Nor had she! All the fellows' heaving at her rope had done was to drag the kedge over the sand.

" She's here till the tide makes!" declared Ron breathlessly. " I hope she won't list too much."

" Aren't there any legs on board?" asked Lofty.

" Haven't seen any," replied Ron.

" Why not use the sweeps?"

" They'll sink in the sand and she'll fall over with a *whump*!" explained the Patrol-leader. " You'd better put that stove out, George, before she lists."

Then, as if to gloat over the Sea Scouts' predicament, the sun shone through the mist and in a few minutes, aided by a gentle breeze, the fog dispersed.

The *Nut* was hard and fast aground a cable's length or more inside the Slimers Buoy!

" How is that?" asked Ned. " I was steering the course you gave me."

" It beats me," admitted Ron. " If it's anyone's fault, it's mine. I worked out the course—and checked it carefully, too!"

They left it at that, and set to work to secure all loose gear before the *Nut* took up her maximum list. This she was rapidly approaching, for already the sands were uncovering for a distance of nearly a mile.

With two exceptions the crew left the yacht and were soon playing rounders on the dry, hard sand. Nick, too, was thoroughly enjoying himself frisking about and fruitlessly chasing the gulls that were searching the pools for fish trapped by the falling tide.

The exceptions were Mr. Miles and Ron.

"I can't think how she got here, sir," said the Patrol-leader.

"Well, cheer up!" rejoined the G.S.M. "Worse things than this happen at sea, and luckily there's no sea on, or she'd bump heavily when she refloats."

"Yes, but two hundred yards out of our course, sir! And I took such care over setting it out."

"Here's the explanation," continued Mr. Miles quietly. "And you needn't mention it to anyone else."

He pointed to some printed lines at the bottom of the chart. They were in such small type that they might easily be overlooked in spite of their importance:

"Mariners are warned that there is a strong indraught into all the bays and bights on this section of the coast. This must be carefully guarded against and in thick weather constant soundings should be taken. Neglect of these precautions has occasioned the loss of several vessels, due to this cause."

" I ought to have seen that, sir," said Ron.

" Well, you know now, my lad! You could have given her another couple of points and then you'd have found yourself outside the buoy. You aren't the first to get a craft aground here, if that's any consolation! And now, I think, we'll lay that kedge out again!"

This they did, taking the precaution of burying it in the sand with a piece of wood against the lowermost fluke.

" That will stop the anchor from dragging," declared the G.S.M. " And when the yacht's over it we can break it out easily enough. Ah! Who's this coming? Not more of our Customs friends to worry us, I hope?"

Trudging over the sand were three men who landed from a boat on the eastern edge of the sands, although their craft was hidden from the *Nut* by the intervening hummocks that had formed over the long-disappeared remains of unfortunate vessels that had ended up upon the treacherous Slimers.

As the men drew nearer—the stranded yacht seemed to be attracting them as a magnet attracts iron—it could be seen that they were carrying nets attached to poles on their shoulders.

"They're after shellfish," declared Ron.

The Sea Scouts stopped their game and could be seen in conversation with the men. Presently the whole party came towards the *Nut.*

"Good afternoon, sir!" began one of the men. "Seems you'm in a pretty mess."

"Not so bad as that, surely!" rejoined Mr. Miles. "She'll float off when the tide makes."

"She may and she may not," continued the man. "Looks to me as if it'll come on to blow from the sou'west. If so, she'll bump her keel out of her afore she lifts. Now look 'ere, sir; me an' my mates 'ave our livin' to earn, but we ain't above lendin' a 'and for a consideration."

"Really?"

"Yes, sir. We'll dig a trench so as she'll slide into it when the flood makes. Then we'll bring our boat round and give her a good pluck off. 'Tes the only way, ain't it, mates?"

"The only way," echoed the other two men lugubriously.

"And it'll only cost you a couple o' pounds, mister!"

"I don't think we need trouble you, thanks," decided Mr. Miles. "The glass is high and steady and what wind there is, is off-shore."

"We've come all this way to lend a hand, and this is what we get!" exclaimed the spokesman truculently.

"We didn't ask you to come," rejoined the G.S.M.

There was a pause, during which the three beach-combers were almost on the point of explosion.

"And there's another thing," resumed the first man. "You'm on a bombing range. As soon as the sands cover—and that'll be afore you'm afloat—them airyplanes'll be over dropping bombs and using machine-guns."

"Yes, I understand that this is an R.A.F. bombing range," agreed Mr. Miles. "But they wouldn't drop bombs on a stranded yacht."

"Wouldn't they? 'Ow could they tell from up there? Only last month a boat was machine-gunned and a man aboard had a shot clean through 'is body. See them buoys?"—he pointed to a couple of small casks with red flags attached—"them's to mark prohibited area; so if you values yer lives you'd best let us gi' ye a 'and to get off!"

"I think we'll risk it," said Mr. Miles coolly. "It'll be rather interesting, if the machines come over, to see what they're doing. Now, don't let us keep you. Time and tide wait for no man, and I'm sure you're anxious to earn a bit by honest fishing."

"'Onest: wot d'yer mean?" demanded the man angrily. "Now, look 'ere, guv'nor; we didn't come 'ere for nothin'."

"You thought we were strangers and therefore easy game," interrupted the G.S.M. sternly. "Now off you go—at once! If you don't I'll call on Captain Jenkins as soon as we arrive at Easthaven!"

The mere mention of the name of the Fisheries Protection Officer was enough. Muttering curses, the three men went off.

"Is this a bombing range, sir?" asked Ned.

"It is."

"Then is it dangerous to be here?"

Mr. Miles smiled.

"Yes, on certain days of the month, but this doesn't happen to be one of them. I looked at the Air Ministry's list of dates in the harbour-master's office before we left Otherport—just in case!"

"I'm awfully glad you came, sir!" confided Ron, as the G.S.M. and the Patrol-leader took a short walk over the sands. "We weren't keen at first, but we were obliged to have someone."

"Meaning me?" rejoined Mr. Miles. "Now look here, Ron, don't take this little mishap too seriously. You might have navigated the *Nut* to Easthaven without the slighest difficulty. The fog was an accident of Nature."

"If I'd seen that notice on the chart——"

"Don't worry about that. After all, it's added to your store of knowledge. We all make mistakes when we're afloat, and there's never a time when the most experienced seaman doesn't learn something fresh. And you'll find very frequently that the fellow who boasts how ably he can manage a craft, whether single-handed or in charge of a crew, generally makes a hash of things at a critical moment. Then he blames everyone and everything except himself.

"Let me tell you a yarn against myself. Not

so long ago I was skippering a motor cruiser bound from Lowestoft to King's Lynn. When off the Norfolk coast I checked her position frequently with landmarks ashore, and to my astonishment and perplexity I found she was doing eight knots against the tide, although her maximum speed was only seven knots. Now, how was that?"

Ron thought for a few moments, then:

" You forgot it was Summer Time, sir, and you were an hour out with your tides?"

" Sorry, you're wrong!" chuckled the G.S.M.

" I give it up, sir!"

" Well, then, you know that on most charts there is a scale of degrees and minutes at all four sides. Those on the east and west are constant, so that a minute of longitude is the same as one sea mile. The chart I was using was different from the usual run, in that the top was east and the sides north and south respectively. I didn't notice that at the time, so that in measuring off the distances I was taking minutes of latitude for those of longitude; thus I was adding roughly one third to the distance actually sailed in any one given time. Now, I won't make that mistake again, though there's no saying how many other bloomers I'll commit before the time comes for me when ' there is no more sea '. Hello! Tide's turned! We should be afloat again in a couple of hours."

The Patrol-leader gave a blast on his whistle, the signal for the stragglers to return, since there might be the risk of some of the party being cut off as the rising waters swirled through the gulleys that intersected the sands.

It was a tedious business. As Ned remarked, "The tide comes in fast enough when you don't want it to, and takes a frightful long time when you do!"

"I wonder what Jakob thinks about his first impression of British soil?" asked Ron.

"Sand—nothing but sand!" exclaimed Lofty. "Here he comes with his flute."

"Flute?" echoed the Patrol-leader.

"Yes, he made it from a bit of cane that was floating in a hole in the sands," explained Lofty. "He borrowed my knife. Plays it jolly well; but none of us can get a sound out of it."

The boy refugee, smiling cheerfully, was certainly proud of his triumph. With only a knife and a piece of bamboo he had fashioned a sort of whistle-pipe from which he could draw a lively lilt.

"Play, Jakob!" prompted Ron.

Without hesitation the young German raised the instrument to his lips and played a lively air.

"Good effort, Jakob!" declared the Patrol-leader, patting the instrumentalist on the back.

"You try, Ron!" suggested Ned. "Bet you you can't!"

Jakob handed Ron the pipe.

In vain the Patrol-leader blew into the mouth-piece until his face was as red as a freshly cut beetroot and the tears were running down his cheeks as the result of his exertions. The more he tried the more the rest of the Troop rocked and yelled with merriment.

"Look at Nick!" exclaimed George. "He's gone dotty!"

When Ron had started his attempt the dog was about a hundred yards off and racing away from the yacht in pursuit of a cormorant. But directly his master commenced to blow through the pipe the animal abandoned the chase and came running towards his master. Almost at Ron's feet he stopped and, throwing back his head, gave vent to a succession of hideous yells.

The Patrol-leader gave Jacob back his pipe and bent over the dog.

"He's thrown a fit!" declared Lofty, but directly Ron put his hand on Nick's head the animal stopped howling and wagged his tail.

"He couldn't stand the noise you made, Ron!" said Lofty.

"Noise? I wasn't making any!" protested Ron. "Besides, if I did, he was too far away to hear."

"Then try again and see what happens," suggested Lofty.

Taking the instrument from Jakob, Ron made yet another effort. Except for the hissing of his breath through the pipe, not a sound could be heard and certainly not a note; but to the Sea Scouts' amazement, Nick cowered and resumed his dolorous howls! Directly his master desisted the dog became normal.

By signs Jakob was asked to play; but the melodious notes appeared to have not the slightest effect upon the animal. Instead, he wandered off to resume his efforts to chase birds.

Again his master put the pipe to his lips and blew through it, though without expecting to produce a note. This time he blew quite gently; but Nick, then quite a distance off, turned and ran back to his master!

"That beats me!" admitted Ron. "He couldn't possibly have heard that!"

"I don't know so much about that," said Ned. "You know Major Green?"

"The dog-breeder who lives near Otherport?"

"Yes. He was telling my father about a silent dog-whistle he'd bought—one that gives such a high-pitched note that human beings can't hear it, but dogs can."

"Did it work all right?" asked Musty.

"Too jolly well," replied Ned. "The

Major gave it away 'cause he said it made him look such a silly ass when people saw him blowing a whistle that didn't give a sound! They must have thought he'd gone batty!"

"Jakob's whistle-pipe made me feel a silly ass anyway," admitted the Patrol-leader. "And it's whacked the lot of us to find out how he does it. Now, all aboard, you fellows! Tide's lapping her keel and it won't be long before she lifts."

The crew clambered on board the steeply listing yacht and perched themselves, at considerable personal discomfort, on the waterways of the higher side.

Two hours had been a very sanguine estimate; actually the flood had been making for nearly three hours before the *Nut* showed signs of tearing herself away from the tenacious embrace of the Slimers Sands.

Surrounded by a swirling mass of muddy water, the yacht lay apparently immovable, with the rising tide lapping her side deck. A few inches more and the water looked like pouring over the cockpit coaming and flooding the little craft. If it did there would be an urgent call for the three beach-combers, since the canvas dinghy couldn't possibly hold more than three of the crew at a time.

Ron found himself wishing that he had taken precautions against the possibility of such a catastrophe. Yachts, he knew, had been lost through being filled with water when lying aground and not lifting in time. He could have tacked waterproof canvas over the cockpit to prevent the inrush, but it would be too late now. Before the job could be completed the tide would have risen another nine inches.

" Slack off the mainsheet and rig a for'ard guy to the boom-end, lads!" he ordered. " Look lively! Ned and Lofty, overboard you go with me and try lifting her!"

Waist-deep in water, the three Sea Scouts grasped the already submerged capping and the chain plates and heaved upward for all they were worth. Then, as soon as the boom was swung outboard, where it tilted up at an angle of about thirty degrees to the horizontal, Musty and George got astride of it, keeping their balance by holding on to the tautened topping-lift. Jakob, tumbling to the idea, joined Mr. Miles in an acrobatic feat of holding on to the shrouds and hanging over the side so that their weight would contribute to the combined lifting efforts of the crew.

Suddenly the *Nut* wrenched herself clear and came up on almost an even keel, but with a slight list in the opposite direction. As she did so the topping lift parted with a twang like the release of a bow-string. There was an ominous splintering of wood, followed by a tremendous splash.

The boom had been completely fractured above the goose-neck and had pitched Musty and George overboard!

Fortunately the water was sufficiently deep to prevent the two youths from sustaining serious injury. Had it been only two or three inches they might have broken their backs upon the hard sand. As it was, they emerged, breathless and spluttering, having swallowed a generous draught of the English Channel but otherwise little the worse.

Ron and his chums also scrambled on board, dripping wet, while Mr. Miles and the German boy, who had saved themselves from a ducking by hanging on to the rigging, were well soused by the splashes sent up by George and Musty.

All this was of slight consequence, as they were lightly clad. What did matter was the broken boom, although that was a relatively small price to pay for saving the *Nut* from becoming a total loss.

The yacht was now bumping lightly. A swell had set in over the sands during the last quarter of an hour and was a sure warning of dirty weather approaching.

"Get the boom inboard, lads!" ordered Ron. "We may be able to fish it. Gently with her!"

The spar, owing to the parting of the topping lift, had fallen with considerable force across the edge of the cabin top, and it was here that the fracture had occurred, roughly three feet from the goose-neck.

As Ned and Musty grasped the broken end, while Ron and Lofty heaved the outer end inboard, the Second slipped and sat down heavily.

"Steady, you lubber!" exclaimed Musty.

"Lubber yourself!" rejoined Ned. "You would have slipped if—I say, Ron, what's this?"

Lying in the waterways were about half a dozen small aluminium cylinders. It was on one of these that Ned's bare foot had slithered.

"Goodness knows!" replied the Patrol-leader.

As he spoke, three more cylinders pattered upon the cabin top and rolled to join the others in the waterways.

"Where did they come from?" asked Ned. "Ah! I see! The boom's hollow! Look, it's stuffed full with them! What are they?"

"Blessed if I know," replied the Patrol-leader. "I say, sir, can you come on deck?"

Mr. Miles, who was changing after his wetting, opened the for'ard skylight.

"What is it?" he asked.

"Look at these things, sir; they fell out of the boom. It's hollow."

Mr. Miles took one of the proffered cylinders.

" I'll be on deck in half a minute!" he announced.

While they were awaiting the G.S.M.'s appearance, the crew examined their find. The cylinders, about four inches in length and an inch in diameter, were sealed with screw stoppers, while underneath the stopper of each was a cork coated with wax. Judging by the dull appearance of the aluminium, the cylinders had been tarnished by the salt air, so that it seemed evident that they had been in their place of concealment for a considerable time.

Presently Mr. Miles came on deck.

" You'd better stop that broken end with a piece of canvas, Ron!" he suggested. " We don't want to lose any of these if we can help it!"

" What are they, sir?" asked the Patrol-leader.

" I can't say with certainty," was the reply. " But now I know why our friend Mr. Badger and all the other Water Guard officers took such a deep interest in the *Nut*!"

" But what, sir——" began Ned.

" Never mind about that now," interrupted the G.S.M. " We'll go into the question when we're under way once more. Get busy, Ron, and I'll make myself scarce."

At the saloon hatchway, Mr. Miles paused.

" None of you fellows has hung on to any of those phials, I hope? If so, hand them to me. We can't encourage souvenir hunting of that sort!"

Each of the crew shook his head. Jakob, guessing the nature of the question, followed their example.

" That's all right, then," continued Mr. Miles. " See that the broken boom-end is properly secured, Ron. We don't want any more of those things to fall all over the deck!"

The *Nut* was now well afloat, and riding by the stern to the kedge. Ahead and on either beam there was considerably less depth of water; so obviously the yacht must come off in the opposite direction to the one in which she had piled herself upon the sands. As frequently happens, owing to the natural perversity of things, the wind was now dead aft, which meant that a beat-out was indicated; although how this could be done with a broken boom was a problem that the Sea-gulls would have to solve for themselves.

"We'd better unlace the mainsail," suggested Ron. "It'll be all right to set it on the run, or with the wind abeam, but beating out with short tacks is going to take a bit of doing!"

"The sail might have been torn," remarked Lofty.

"It might," agreed the Patrol-leader. "Let's see. Now, you others, bring the warp for'ard outside of everything, and let her swing to it!"

It did not take long to unlace the mainsail from the two unequal portions of the fractured boom. Luckily the foot-rope had stood the strain, so that the canvas was neither torn nor unduly stretched. The boom was then laid along the waterways and securely lashed down, after especial care had been taken to plug the ends so that no more of the aluminium cylinders could escape.

"I don't think Mr. Gunville knows anything about it," declared Ned, standing up for the benefactor who had given the *Dark Secret*—the motor cruiser they had not yet seen—to the Otherport Sea Scouts. "I reckon those chaps who tried to board us had planted the things there."

" When?" asked Musty.

" Might be before he bought the *Nut*; or they may have made a mistake——"

" They certainly did!" interrupted George.

" Made a mistake," continued Ned, ignoring the interruption, " and stowed the things on board while he was away."

" That was no reason why they should slosh Mr. Gunville over the head," observed Lofty. " There's more in this than meets the eye. Why hadn't he set a reefed mainsail before we took her in tow to Otherport?"

" He'd sprained his wrist, of course," replied Ned.

" I'd hoist that sail with one hand," persisted Lofty. " No, I reckon he was afraid of the boom parting and chucking those cylinders into the ditch!"

" You may think what you like——" began Ned.

" Stop arguing there!" ordered Ron. " Everything ready? Right-o! Start her up, Musty!"

As soon as the motor was running and had warmed up sufficiently to prevent an accidental stop when it had to take up the load, Ron cast off the kedge rope aft. Almost at once the *Nut* began to swing—the Patrol-leader had seen to it that she would do so clear of the again tautened rope—and brought up with a jerk head to wind and with her bows pointing down the gulley leading to deep water.

" Up with the kedge, lads!" ordered Ron. " Get the warp in by hand. It's quicker than using the winch!"

Three of the crew on the fore-deck heaved away at the grass rope. Steadily the yacht forged ahead until she was over the kedge; and then, in spite of their united efforts, the trio could not break the " hook " out of the sand.

" We've buried it too deep!" declared George. " It'll mean the winch after all!"

They took two or three turns of the rope round the drum of the winch, George being told off to take the strain, then——

" Where's the winch handle, Lofty?" asked Ned.

Lofty shook his head.

" I never saw it," he declared.

" What's up, there?" inquired Ron, who was standing by the tiller.

" No winch handle, Captain!"

" It should be underneath the winch and made fast by a piece of line!"

" The line's there but no handle," announced Ned. " It must have carried away."

" We could use a spanner with a piece of iron pipe as an extension handle," suggested Lofty. " There's one in the tool locker. I'll fetch it!"

"It'll be too slow a job," objected Ned. "Take a strain on the warp! Now, everybody aft. Put her ahead, Musty."

It seemed a tough proposition for so small an engine; but, aided by the slight swell, the motor did what was required of it. Out came the kedge, which was soon unbent from the warp and stowed away.

By this time the *Nut* was in deep water, but not until Ron had taken a compass bearing of the buoy marking the extremity of the sand, and found that he had an ample margin of safety, did he alter helm and steer seawards.

He wasn't going to try conclusions with the Slimers a second time, even though there was now sufficient water over the sands!

As soon as the yacht was on her course for Easthaven, the wind now being two points abaft the beam, the sails were hoisted and the motor switched off.

Although the mainsail bagged considerably, for without the boom it could not be properly sheeted home, it took the yacht along at a fair pace without any appreciable strain upon the helmsman.

"Tea's ready!" sang out George.

"'Bout time too!" rejoined Lofty. "Heaving and hauling have made my throat as dry as a bone! I couldn't eat a thing until——"

Ron took him at his word and cut short the rest of the sentence.

"Splendid!" he exclaimed. "If you're not hungry you can take the tiller and we'll pass you out a mug of nice hot tea!"

"What's in those things, sir?" asked Ned, as the rest of the crew sat down at the saloon table. "Are they incendiary bombs?"

"Or poisonous germs, sir?" added George.

"Neither, but something equally dangerous, I imagine. They contain cocaine or some similar drug. At any rate, I'm not going to sample them; I'll leave that to the Customs officers."

"Has Mr. Gunville anything to do with them?" asked Musty, who shared Lofty's suspicions concerning the owner of the *Nut*.

"That I won't say," replied the G.S.M. "It's not fair to cast aspersions on a man who isn't here to defend himself. But what we do know is that the Customs have their suspicions concerning the yacht and these are certainly not unfounded. And what's more, there's a gang at work trying to remove the stuff before the *Nut* makes Easthaven—those two fellows who came on board the night before we left Otherport, and the crowd in the two motor launches who wanted to set us ashore and tow the yacht into Easthaven, or rather, said that's what they'd been instructed to do. If we had taken them at their word they would have removed the drug—apparently they knew where it was hidden—and scuttled the yacht in deep water. So now it looks as if there's going to be some more excitement for us when we make Easthaven. Technically we're smugglers, lads!"

"I'm glad you think Mr. Gunville isn't mixed up with the smugglers," said Ned. "He wouldn't have given us the *Dark Secret* if he had been. But, I say, sir!"

"What is it?"

"We haven't anything to show the man in charge of her that she's ours."

"I understand that he wrote to the shipyard where the cruiser is lying," said Mr. Miles. "There are no 'papers', so she isn't registered. We mustn't expect too much. Isn't there a proverb about looking a gift horse in the mouth?"

"It's a pity we didn't look carefully at the *Venture* when we bought her," added Ron. "More tea, Jakob?"

The German youth smiled, nodded and replied "*Iss.*"

"Getting on with the language, isn't he, sir?" remarked Ned. "It must be a bit rotten for him, with all this talk going on and he can't make head or tail of it. But it isn't much use for him to learn English if he's going to be hoofed out of it. What with Jakob and the dope, we're going to have a busy day."

"That won't be till to-morrow," declared Ron. "Wind's falling light. It'll be dark before we arrive, at this rate. Honestly, I don't like the idea of taking the yacht into a strange harbour at night."

"Why should we?" asked Ned. "Glass is high and steady, and our friends the beachcombers seem to be considerably out in their forecast. Can't we bring up outside, as we did off Dockingham?"

Ron looked inquiringly at the Scoutmaster, but Mr. Miles feigned interest elsewhere. Since no hazardous situation was at stake, it was for the Patrol-leader to make the decision.

"All right," he replied. "We'll make another night of it."

Actually it was eleven o'clock before the *Nut* brought the leading lights of Easthaven in line. Working inshore till the soundings gave only two fathoms at low water, the yacht brought up to her own anchor and kedge.

Unlike Dockingham, Easthaven has a busy trade, not only by means of coastal shipping but with continental ports. So when Ron saw the constant procession of navigation lights as vessels large and small were either leaving or berthing at tide-time, he was glad he had decided not to risk entering the crowded harbour, where pleasure craft are few in number and not particularly welcomed by the harbour authorities.

By choosing an anchorage inside the five-fathom line and well clear of the fairway, he knew that there was little or no risk of being run down in the night owing to the carelessness of a helmsman or to the accidental extinguishing of the yacht's riding-light.

"We'll keep anchor-watch, of course," announced Ron to the crew. "Two-hour tricks between three of us. That'll see us through till sunrise."

George stifled a yawn.

"I don't mind," he declared. "But I hope I don't get the second shift. Mucks up a fellow's sleep."

"It's going to be fair does," continued the Patrol-leader. "We'll draw for it. The fellow who draws the shortest piece is the first to go on watch; the second shortest piece goes next, and so on. I'll cut, and you'll draw, George!"

With that Ron cut five slips of plain paper, each equal in width but of different lengths. These he slipped inside an empty match box, turning his back to his chums as he did so, leaving the exposed ends showing evenly.

"Youngest first," he announced. "Draw for George, Ned!"

"Well, you're all right for a good sleep, George," exclaimed the Second. "Now, who's next?"

The result of the ballot showed that Ron was to take the first spell of anchor-watch,

Lofty being second and Musty third. George and Ned, having the two longest slips, were exempt altogether.

" So that's that!" exclaimed Ron, as he lifted his oilskin from its hook. " Thank goodness it's a warm, clear night. Well, night-night, you fellows. I'll hoof you out at two o'clock, Lofty!"

Left to himself in the cockpit, Ron brought out a couple of fishing lines, baiting the hooks with pieces of bacon fat. He knew this was by no means the ideal bait, but since he hadn't either rag- or lug-worm—he felt like kicking himself for not digging for some during the long hours the *Nut* had been left high and dry on the Slimers—he had to make use of the next best thing.

He had hardly let the sinker of the first line touch bottom when he became aware of a distinct tremble. He knew what that meant —the line was vibrating in the tide-way—and did not fall into the error that so many amateur fishermen make, that he had a bite.

About half an hour later there was a distinct though unmistakable jerk of the line. Ron did not attempt to " strike ". It was only a nibble, and until the fish had taken the hook inside its mouth there was little chance of the barbed point obtaining a hold.

But when the Patrol-leader did haul up the line he was pleasurably astonished to find not one but two fairly large flounders securely hooked.

By the time the Town Hall clock had boomed out the hour of one, Ron had a dozen goodly fish flopping on the stern-sheet grating; and since his supply of bait was exhausted he decided to suspend operations, especially as there was enough and to spare for breakfast.

Drawing his oilskin tighter, for a heavy dew was falling, Ron prepared to spend the second hour of his trick in comparative inaction. There was nothing much to be done. The riding-light was burning brightly and the yacht was showing no signs of dragging her anchor. The illuminated face of the Town Hall clock was in line with and over the green lamp on the inner end of the east pier, as they had been when he first went on watch. It was now approaching slack water. Before his "trick" was up the yacht would have swung and be riding to her kedge anchor.

Suddenly Ron pricked up his ears. He could hear the faint plash of oars—fishermen, probably, putting out to their night's work. It couldn't be the crew of a vessel, since there was no other craft of any description anchored in the open roadstead.

The sound of the oars drew nearer and louder, and presently Ron could discern a boat manned by a couple of men making straight for the *Nut*.

As the rowers had their backs turned away from him Ron thought he might just as well give them a hail, so that they could avoid running into the yacht.

"Ahoy!" he called, moderating his voice, so as not to disturb his sleeping chums.

The men lay on their oars until the boat, still carrying way, was within a couple of oars' length of the yacht's quarter. Then, one of the men backing his oar, the boat swung round and came gently alongside.

"So you've arrived?" began one of the men.

"You're expecting us?"

"We're expecting the *Nut.* Gunville wrote and told us that some Sea Scouts were bringing her from Otherport. You are a Sea Scout?"

"Rather!"

"Good for you! Why didn't you come into the harbour instead of bringing up out here?"

"We thought we'd better wait till daylight," explained Ron. "We're strangers here. Besides, we don't want to be bothered by the Customs at this time of night."

"Customs? They won't trouble you. All they'll want to know is whether you're from a foreign port, which you aren't! We'll tow you in, if you like—the tide's getting slack so it'll be an easy job—and put you on the *Nut's* own moorings. Then I can telegraph to

Gunville the first thing in the morning and tell him you've arrived safely. I know he'll be anxious until he knows she's back."

"Thanks all the same," replied Ron. "The rest of the fellows are asleep and it's a shame to turn them out. And Mr. Miles wouldn't like to be disturbed."

"Who's Mr. Miles?"

"Our Scoutmaster; didn't you know he is on board?"

"Just as you like," rejoined the man in the boat, who had been the only one who had taken part in the conversation. "We came out just in case. No matter; it's a fine night and a little exercise won't do us any harm. See you in the morning. By the way, you know where her moorings are?"

"No, I'm afraid I don't."

"Straight up the harbour, through the swing bridge—that'll open for you—and up the first creek to starboard. Channel's marked by black posts to port and black-and-white to starboard, so you can't make any mistake. A quarter of a mile up you'll see Bickerdyke's boat-yard on your port hand. *Nut's* moorings are just opposite—a red buoy with her name on it. But we'll be there on the look-out for you. Well, good night!"

"Good night, and thank you," returned the Patrol-leader.

The boat disappeared into the darkness.

"Jolly decent of them to offer to tow us in," thought Ron. "Friends of Mr. Gunville's, I suppose. I wish I'd asked them about the *Dark Secret*, whether she's on moorings or hauled out at the boat-yard."

The rest of the second hour passed without incident, and at ten minutes past—Ron wasn't going to show his "relief" that he'd been so keen as all that to finish his trick dead on time—he went quietly into the saloon and turned Lofty out of his bunk.

"What's it like outside?" asked Lofty in a whisper.

"Not so bad! Mind where you step when you go out. There's about a dozen fish lying on the grating!"

"Fish? Gosh! I'll have a go!"

"You'll have to find some bait. I used bacon fat. I don't know whether George has any left."

They searched the galley with the aid of a carefully screened torch, but without the desired result.

"Tell you what," suggested Lofty, now fully awake and eager to get down to business. "We can cut up one of the fish you caught."

"All right," agreed Ron. "And I'll string the rest of my catch together so they won't get mixed up with yours! Lead on, Macduff!"

But before the two lads could gain the cockpit, a bellowing voice, utterly regardless of the obvious fact that part at least of the crew were asleep, boomed out:

"Yacht ahoy! Where are you from?"

CHAPTER XXI

THE NET CLOSES

The strident hail brought all the sleepers from their bunks. Ron pitched his catch into a beaker only just in time. Even Jakob joined in the rush of dishevelled lads on deck. Possibly he thought that the yacht was in imminent danger of being sunk.

Mr. Miles, too, came out by way of the fore-hatch, so that he stood alone in his pyjamas on the fore-deck.

"Yacht *Nut*," replied Ron. "From Otherport!"

"Ah!"

There was a tone of satisfaction in that monosyllable.

"What are you doing here?" inquired a white-uniform-capped officer in the stern-sheets of the motor boat, whose engines, though still running, were hardly audible.

"Waiting for daylight, sir!"

"Had any communication with the shore?"

"Yes, a boat came alongside us half an hour ago."

"A-ha! And a good thing for you you

admitted it! Any of your crew went ashore in her?"

"No."

"Did she take anything off from the yacht?"

"No; there were two gentlemen in her—friends of the owner, Mr. Gunville—and they offered to tow us in and put us on the *Nut's* own moorings."

"Did they?" rejoined the Water Guard officer, with a dry laugh. "We'll want to have a look at you before then!"

It was about time, thought Mr. Miles, that he put his oar in.

"Isn't it most unreasonable of you to disturb these lads of mine at this unearthly hour of the night?" he inquired. "Perhaps you are not aware that this yacht has been 'rummaged'—I think that's what you term it—at Otherport and again off Dockingham."

"And we're going to search her again, sir," persisted the Customs officer. "We have our suspicions, but that's not to say you're mixed up in this business. We've our duty to do, sir!"

"That I'm not disputing, but there's a time for everything."

"If you were in the Water Guard, sir, you'd find the time for everything means every blessed minute of the hour and every hour of the twenty-four!"

"Then I'm glad I'm not," rejoined the

G.S.M. heartily. " As a matter of fact, it is my intention to report to you directly we enter the harbour, and not outside in the fairway."

" Report what, sir?"

" Oh, a certain incident that occurred on our way round, but it'll keep till nine to-morrow!"

The Water Guard officer appeared to consider the statement. As he did so, he flashed his lamp over the cockpit and into the faces of the lads standing there.

" No need to blubber, sonny!" exclaimed the officer. " We're not going to hurt you. What's upset your apple cart?"

Jakob did not reply, for the simple reason that he didn't understand the questions. All he knew was that the man was wearing a uniform, and that put it into his head that he had been signalled out to be arrested.

" So this boy's a foreigner?" inquired the Water Guard officer.

" Yes, a German refugee. We picked him up after he had jumped overboard from a passing vessel. So, you see, we have something of importance to report. Now, with your permission we'll turn in, and I'll give you my word to report at the Custom House directly after our arrival."

" I'll have to leave a man aboard you," decided the officer.

" Just as you like," agreed Mr. Miles. " Only I'd like to point out that we've no accommodation below for him. If he's put in charge, so much the better for us. We can all turn in and get some sleep!"

There was a whispered conversation between the crew of the launch. They hadn't any control over the foreign refugee until he set foot on shore; while the boatman detailed for the job of watchman on the yacht explained to his superior officer that he hadn't had a meal since he came on duty and he hadn't brought any grub with him.

"Very good, sir!" said the Water Guard officer, addressing the Scoutmaster. "If you give me your word—and I know a Scout's word is to be trusted, my boy being a Scout—that you won't hold any communication with the shore, we'll sheer off. I'll send out and have you towed in at eight."

"Done!" agreed Mr. Miles.

"Right! Then we'll push off. Sorry to have disturbed you fellows, but duty's duty, you know!"

The motor launch gathered way, her steaming lights disappearing from view as she did so.

"Now turn in, you fellows!" ordered the G.S.M. briskly. "No yarning, or you'll be too bat-eyed in the morning to enjoy the performance."

With the exception of Lofty the others went below. Although it was some time before all of them were asleep, they felt no resentment at being turned out by the visit of the Customs. That had happened before, so that it might have become monotonous; but this time there promised to be great excitement in its wake!

Well before eight o'clock the Sea Scouts had washed, " shifted " into uniform and had had breakfast. All they now had to do was to await the arrival of the motor launch.

" All merry and bright, I see!" was the Water Guard officer's greeting.

His attitude, compared with that of the previous night, seemed to have undergone a complete change. Perhaps, as Ned suggested, the fact that he had been turned out in the darkness to put off to the yacht had made him a bit liverish; but now his weather-beaten face was beaming.

" We're quite all right, thank you, sir," replied Ron.

" That's good! Now, get your anchor up and we'll be off!"

Actually there were two anchors to be weighed and stowed, but, without getting their uniforms caked with mud, the Seagulls carried out the operation in quick time.

Then, in tow of the Customs launch and with the Scouts' burgee flying proudly from the masthead—probably for the last time—the *Nut* glided between the pier-heads of Easthaven Harbour.

As usual there were quite a number of people about, mostly seafarers and 'longshore-men, with a fair sprinkling of holiday-makers, and the sight of the little yacht being brought in by the Water Guard gave rise to many highly coloured rumours.

Leaving their car parked behind the fish market, two well-dressed men watched the *Nut* being brought alongside the Customs watch-house slipway. Ron, had he seen them, would have had no hesitation in recognizing them as the pair who put off to the yacht during the night. Instead of waiting, as they had announced, at Bickerdyke's boat-yard to see the *Nut* pick up her moorings, they had anticipated her arrival by motoring down to the harbour.

Having seen that the yacht was, so to speak, under arrest, they just looked at each other without speaking a word. Then, returning to their car, they shook the dust of Easthaven from their feet—and their tyres—stopping at the next village to send off a telegram bearing, in addition to the name and address of the person for whom it was intended, one word: " Oppit ".

" Now, what about this young foreigner?" asked the Water Guard officer when the *Nut* was safely berthed. " We'll have to hand him over to the police and he'll be brought before the magistrates at eleven."

"I suppose so," agreed Mr. Miles. "And I'd like to attend the court."

"There's nothing that I know of to prevent you."

"Precisely. There'll be an interpreter? The boy is ignorant of English."

"The police are bound to see to that."

"But couldn't the interpreter be brought here before the lad is taken away? It seems hard on him to be hustled off by the police, not knowing why."

"Yes, I see your point. I'll ring up the Chief Constable."

"Thanks awfully," replied the Group Scoutmaster. "And there's another little point I'd like to raise."

"You seem bristling with them," rejoined the Customs officer genially. "Well, fire away!"

"You intend to make another search of the yacht, I understand. Have you any objection to our saving you that trouble by handing over a quantity of cocaine?"

"Cocaine!" exclaimed the other excitedly. "Good heavens! You don't say so. Where is it?"

"Here's the first instalment," announced Mr. Miles, producing one of the aluminium cylinders from his pocket.

"That's the stuff, right enough. Seen these neat little cartons before. Buy 'em on the other side for a few hundred francs a gross, and they'll fetch anything up to ten pounds an ounce here, if they get past us. Where's the rest?"

The G.S.M. pointed to the boom lying along the waterways.

" Hollow and chock full of it," he declared.

" That's evidence all right," added the Water Guard officer. " Hi, you! Bear a hand and cart this spar to No. 3 shed and ask Mr. Conolly to step this way! Now, sir, if you'll give me a statement I'll take it down, and then you'll sign it. I suppose none of these lads have any of the stuff in their possession?"

" That I'm certain of."

" Good! Now, before you make your declaration I'll ring up the Chief Constable and ask him to take out a warrant. We know who our man is, and we've been waiting a jolly sight too long; but we've got him all right this time!"

CHAPTER XXII

"CAUGHT!"

"How goes it this morning?" inquired Scoutmaster Dyson, as he carefully lowered himself into a deck chair on the sunny veranda of the Princess Margaret Hospital at Otherport.

"Nothing much to complain about," replied Tarrant Gunville, who was already reclining in an adjacent chair. "Head still throbs a bit, but that's not to be wondered at. Thank goodness I can smoke."

Slowly he refilled the bowl of his pipe and then proffered his pouch to his companion.

"Thanks, no," replied Dyson. "Not just yet. The fresh air's good enough to go on with! Topping morning, isn't it? Those young rascals of mine are lucky in the weather for their trip round. Wish I'd been fit enough to go with them; it was awfully decent of Miles to take over almost at a moment's notice."

He gazed over the sunlit harbour. The fishing-fleet was making its way home; some of the trawlers were shooting between the pier-heads. Outside, the sea was dotted with the white sails of half a dozen small yachts. On the mud left bare with the falling tide gulls were strutting, suddenly stopping to pick up their morning meal, or wheeling round lazily in the air with the utmost confidence. No man or boy belonging to Otherport would deliberately harm a gull, and the birds seemed to know!

" Yes, it was good of him," remarked Gunville, after a pause.

" And jolly sporting of you to give the Sea Scouts the *Dark Secret*. I hope you know how that is appreciated."

Tarrant Gunville made a deprecating gesture with his hand.

" It's nothing, really," he protested. " I'm not using her and she'd only go to wrack and ruin where she is. Far better for her to be used. I warned you she'd require refitting, but in her present condition there's no reason why they shouldn't bring her here almost as soon as they arrive at Easthaven."

" You haven't heard whether they've arrived there yet?"

" No; have you?"

Dyson shook his head.

" Miles would wire to you first, I should think," he replied. " And I would have to wait for a letter from him. All the same, it's quite about time one or other of us heard. When are you leaving?"

" Next Saturday, I hope. That is, if the

doctor will let me, and I think there's every probability that he will. I've arranged for some friends of mine to fetch me by car and then I'm going to their place in Surrey to recuperate. Hang it all, Dyson, I wish you were coming along too! There's nothing like a complete change of air to buck a fellow up after an operation."

" Thanks; but I must get back to my job," replied the Scoutmaster. " I'm not a man of leisure."

" If it comes to that——" began Mr. Gunville.

" Here's a telegram for you, Mr. Gunville!" announced a nurse who had just come through the open french window.

She handed him the orange-coloured envelope and stepped back beyond the chair in which Dyson was reclining.

The S.M. noticed that Gunville's hand trembled as he slit open the flap, but perhaps that shakiness was a natural result of his head injuries.

" I say: bad news!" ejaculated Gunville, looking really agitated.

" Anything happened to the *Nut*?" asked Dyson.

" No, nothing about her; my father's dangerously ill. I'll have to go at once, whatever the doctor says. Give me a lift up, please, Nurse!"

" I say, I am sorry!" exclaimed Dyson sympathetically.

Gunville made no audible reply. With deliberate precision he folded the telegram and placed it in the pocket of his dressing-gown and went back to his room.

A quarter of an hour later he was fully dressed. A taxi had been ordered and the departing patient was saying good-bye to the matron.

" I'm frightfully grateful to you, Matron!" he exclaimed. " And the staff have been wonderful. My opinion of the nursing profession rises higher and higher! I'm afraid that in my present state of agitation I cannot adequately express my thanks. And how much am I indebted to the hospital for treatment?"

" This is a voluntarily supported hospital and treatment is free," explained the Matron. " But, of course, in most cases, if the patients can afford it, they make a voluntary contribution according to their means and the extent of their gratitude!"

" Then shall we say twenty guineas? I have every reason to be grateful."

" The almoner would be delighted, Mr. Gunville."

" Right! She shall have it! I haven't my cheque book with me, but a cheque will be sent within the next few days. Good-bye and thank you!"

The matron, a sister and two nurses accompanied the departing patient as far as the vestibule. There, declining an offer by one of the nurses to carry his suitcase to the entrance gates, Gunville again thanked everybody and went.

He had made himself rather popular with those of the staff with whom he had come in contact.

He didn't hurry. His legs, unused to exercise, felt as if they were giving way. But there was no need for immediate haste. His train would not leave for another twenty-five minutes.

The porter wasn't on duty, but his wife opened the heavy iron gates. Gunville stepped on to the pavement, against which the taxi was waiting. Rather petulantly he asked himself why it hadn't come to the hospital entrance instead of stopping there. It would have saved him a walk of about a hundred yards.

The taximan got off his seat and came round to open the door.

At that moment two men in bowler hats, looking like well-to-do farmers, stepped behind the fare.

"Are you Mr. Tarrant Gunville?" asked one quietly.

"Yes?"

"We are police officers, Mr. Gunville. We

have a warrant for your arrest on a charge of attempted smuggling. It is my duty to warn you that any statement you make may be used in evidence!"

Gunville kept his mouth shut. Unostentatiously, so that none of the passers-by realized what was transpiring, the two plain-clothes detectives ushered their prisoner into the waiting vehicle.

The taximan let in his clutch. He hadn't to be told his destination!

The clocks were striking nine.

There was a special sitting of the Easthaven magistrates at eleven that same morning. Events had moved rapidly since the *Nut* had been brought into her home port, and in spite of reticence on the part of the police and other officials, the news had spread abroad that Tarrant Gunville, a well-known local yachtsman, was due to appear before the bench on a serious charge. In consequence, the court-room was packed almost to suffocation point by a throng composed mainly of the unwashed of the town.

Mr. Miles and Ron Bradley were present as witnesses—not against Tarrant Gunville, for in his case the police asked for sufficient evidence only in order to obtain the prisoner's remand—but in a case that was now the first to be taken, against Jakob Schoffler, an alien who had attempted to land without a permit.

The police had dealt with the business most considerately. An interpreter had been found and a solicitor had appeared on behalf of the accused, who seemed quite bewildered, wondering what it was all about. He had been given to understand that once he set foot in England he would be free, and instead he found himself in charge of a policeman, who, however, treated him kindly.

After Mr. Miles and the Patrol-leader had given evidence, the defending solicitor arose and addressed the Bench.

"I have obtained my client's story from the interpreter now in Court, your worships, and I can most emphatically declare that this is one of the most painful cases it has been my lot to defend. Jakob—I cannot hope to pronounce his surname—is the only son of an eminent doctor living in a town in East Germany, now incorporated within Soviet-occupied Germany. Jakob saw his father arrested and taken off to an unknown destination. Probably he will never see him again. His mother, frantic at the blow, became demented, and Jakob does not know what happened to her. All he did know was that his parents' house was ransacked and that similar brutal treatment was being meted out to everyone in the town suspected of having anti-Soviet sympathies. This young German, with others, was ejected from the town of his birth. The new frontier was closed to them. They eked out a pitiable existence by feeding on the growing produce of the fields.

"At length—and I will not take up too

much of the Court's time by relating his adventures and hardships—Jakob found his way through to a Baltic port, where he contrived to secrete himself on board a timber-carrying vessel bound for England, where he fondly hoped to find an asylum and liberty."

The magistrates conferred amongst themselves and then the chairman spoke:

" While quite in sympathy with this unfortunate youth and with his persecuted race in general, the Bench have their duty to perform. Under the laws of the Realm we are of the considered opinion that we have no option but to recommend Jakob——" He paused, peered at a paper before him and then handed it to his neighbour, who, after looking at it, shook his head.

" —To recommend this German subject for deportation."

Jakob's solicitor was on his feet again.

" Your worships!" he exclaimed, " it is not for me to question the ruling of this Court, neither am I asking for that leniency that the law of this country shows to aliens who are neither criminals nor undesirables. But I would remind you that under the recently amended regulations, deportation is not applicable to persons under the age of sixteen years."

The chairman whispered to the clerk, who nodded his head.

"How old is this—er—youth?" asked the clerk.

"He will tell you himself," replied the solicitor.

There was a brief conversation between the interpreter and Jakob, then the young refugee held up the fingers of both hands followed by those of his right.

"He declares he's fifteen, your worships."

"No more? He looks quite eighteen to me!" declared the Senior Magistrate. "But in absence of evidence to the contrary it affords me much pleasure to order the accused to be discharged from custody, subject to some person of substance holding himself responsible for this refugee's maintenance and guaranteeing that he will not be chargeable to the rates."

Without hesitation Mr. Miles stepped into the well of the Court.

"I will undertake that responsibility, your worships!"

"Your name?"

"Peter Kenneth Miles."

"Profession or occupation?"

"Independent — Scoutmaster by inclination!"

"And we can ask for no better recommendation," rejoined the Chairman. "Thank you, Mr. Miles. After the Court has risen I'd like a few words with you."

The interpreter spoke to Jakob, who, to the amusement of everyone, gave the Scout salute, not to the Bench but to a portly sergeant of police! Then he followed the G.S.M. to the seats reserved for witnesses.

"Silence in Court!" ordered the usher, and the Clerk followed by "Next case, please!"

Every neck was craned and every pair of eyes fixed upon the door through which Tarrant Gunville was to be brought in. But the interested spectators were disappointed, for the whole proceedings lasted barely three minutes and the accused, as was expected, was remanded for seven days, bail being refused. The Chief Constable of Easthaven was taking no risks, especially in view of the fact that a telegram had been found on the prisoner bearing the significant word "Oppit"!

"What price the *Dark Secret* now, sir?" asked Ron, when, with Jakob keeping close to his new guardian, Mr. Miles was on his way back to the yacht *Nut*.

"I hardly like to venture an opinion," replied the G.S.M. "But, after we've packed up, we'll go along to Bickerdyke's boat-yard and see how the land lies, so to speak."

"What's happened, sir?" asked the rest of the patrol in unison, when they arrived back.

"Mr. Gunville's remanded for a week, and

after that, I suppose he'll be committed to the Assizes."

"Yes; but Jakob?"

"He's staying on with me," replied Mr. Miles. "We'll have to buy a German-English phrase book to get on with until he learns English. I expect you'll see quite a lot of him at Otherport! Well, are you ready? Everything packed and the ship left spick and span?"

"Ned saw to that," replied Lofty with a grin. "Kept us at it like niggers all the time you were away."

"We've an hour and a half before the train leaves," announced Mr. Miles.

"Train, sir? We thought we were bringing back the *Dark Secret*?"

"'Fraid that's off, in view of present regrettable circumstances," said the G.S.M. "But we'll go and have a look at her before we leave."

Rather regretfully, the Sea Scouts went ashore. In spite of difficulties, they had had an exciting though all too brief a voyage in the sturdy little *Nut*, even though they had been packed like sardines in a tin.

"So you're off, Mr. Miles!" exclaimed the senior officer of the Water Guard when the departing crew stopped to hand over the yacht's keys. "We'll be seeing you again in a week."

"Yes, unfortunately," admitted the Scoutmaster. "I suppose they'll want my evidence, but I've arranged for Ron Bradley to be excused attendance. And after that the Assizes. What do you think he'll get?"

"Five years, and he deserves it," replied the officer. "And, of course, the yacht will be confiscated and sold—not that he'd be likely to use her awhile! I suppose you know that your Sea Scouts are entitled to a *per centum* of the value of the smuggled goods?"

"No, I didn't!"

"Well, they are, and they might just as well have it as let the Government have it! 'Them's my sentiments though I say it as shouldn't'," he quoted. "The Income Tax people never let you know what deductions you are entitled to, but let you find out for yourself if you can! And it's the same with our Department."

"We'll bear your advice in mind," rejoined Mr. Miles, as he shook hands with the genial and comforting Water Guard officer. "Now what is the way to Bickerdyke's yard?"

Following the directions given, it took the Sea Scouts exactly eight minutes to reach the place, which consisted of an office, three sheds, a couple of slipways and a hard running down to low-water mark. In the stream were some half a dozen yachts on moorings and an unoccupied buoy on which the name *Nut* was visible.

"Are you Mr. Bickerdyke?" asked the G.S.M., addressing a burly, good-natured man who had come from one of the sheds.

"At your service, sir."

"My name's Miles, not that it will convey anything to you. What we've come for is to see a motor cruiser we're interested in."

"The *Magnet*?" asked the boat-yard proprietor hopefully.

"No, the *Dark Secret*."

"Oh! She used to belong to that chap Gunville who was up before the Bench this morning."

"Used to?"

"Yes; she's owned by a Mr. Peter Walsh. Gunville sold her a couple of months back; leastways, he handed her over to Mr. Walsh on account of money owing which he couldn't get otherwise!"

"But Mr. Gunville, while he was in hospital at Otherport, promised her to the Otherport Sea Scouts. I understand he wrote to you, giving you authority to let us take her away."

Mr. Bickerdyke smiled.

"Just like his nerve! For one thing, he didn't write to me. He knew I was off on my fortnight's holiday, but I had to cut 'en short and get back last Saturday. And Mr. Walsh is away for a month."

"Then what was his idea? We brought

the *Nut* round for him with the idea that we should be given the *Dark Secret* and go home in her."

"Another of his shady tricks, I'll allow. You bring the *Nut* here, he thinking I'm away and only my boy Joe looking after things. Then his pals will remove the smuggled stuff——"

"How did you know there was contraband on board?"

"All Easthaven knows now," continued the boat-yard proprietor. "Then directly the stuff's taken off you'll bet your boots Gunville would have made a complete fade-out if the police hadn't nabbed him. It wouldn't surprise me to learn that he's been trying to sell the *Nut* and some simpleton—you know what some yachtsmen are!—has made a fat deposit on her already! And he owes me a matter of close on twenty pounds! Until I heard he'd been collared by the police I thought he was a gentleman!"

"That's hard lines," commented Mr. Miles, glancing at his wrist-watch. "I suppose you have no objection to our having a look at the *Dark Secret*?"

"You're welcome, sir; and I reckon Mr. Walsh won't mind either! She's a bit too big for him, and if there's a likely customer he's open to an offer."

The *Dark Secret* was lying hauled up under

G 715

"I WILL UNDERTAKE THAT RESPONSIBILITY"

Page 233

a covered slipway. Judging by her appearance, she had been there a long time, but her hull, in spite of blistered paint and the deficiency of it in places, seemed to be sound. She was about thirty-five feet in length, with ample accommodation although roughly constructed, while her engine, a 25 horse-power four-cylinder motor, looked decidedly superior to the rest of the equipment.

"A good little engine and economical," declared Mr. Bickerdyke. "Runs on paraffin, too!"

"Wouldn't she make a decent Troop cruiser, sir!" exclaimed Ron, when the Sea Scouts were on their way to the railway station.

"She would," agreed Mr. Miles. "The craft you fellows might have had, but didn't!"

Still smiling, though naturally disappointed, the Seagulls arrived at Otherport station, where they separated, each going to his home.

There were plenty of anecdotes to be told, but generally the story of Tarrant Gunville's bad faith towards the Otherport Sea Scouts was treated lightly by the lads who had been directly affected.

They had been " left high and dry ", as it were. They were without a boat of any description—if one omits the rot-infected hull of the old *Venture*—and, so far, were without funds to buy another. The best thing they could do, it seemed, was to spend what little they had in a doubtful effort to make the *Venture* seaworthy. A Sea Scout Troop, without something to go afloat in, was unthinkable!

A fortnight passed. Mr. Miles had to make another journey to Easthaven as a witness in the Tarrant Gunville case. As was expected, the accused was committed for trial at the autumn Assizes.

Then, quite unexpectedly, the fortunes of the Otherport Sea Scouts began to change, when " Bungs " Cotter informed them that he had an offer for the *Venture*, " as she now lies ", from a local fisherman.

" He's willing to give ten pounds for her," said the boat-builder. " He knows what she's like and so he ain't buying a pig in a poke. I reckon you'll do well to jump at the offer!"

This the Sea Scouts did, and that was the end of the *Venture*, as far as they were concerned.

Next came news that two individuals well known to the police had been arrested on a charge of causing bodily harm to Tarrant Gunville. Apparently, though there may be honour between thieves, there is often precious little between dope smugglers.

Consequently when Spike Dawkins and William Gubbins, known to his associates as The Grubber, were remanded for a week and then committed to the Assizes, they employed part of the interval in telling all they knew concerning the felonious activities of Tarrant Gunville.

According to them—and this supported various theories held by Her Majesty's Customs although they had not been able to confirm their suspicions until the return of the *Nut* to Easthaven—Gunville had been using the yacht for a considerable time as a medium for bringing large supplies of illegal drugs into the country.

His method was very simple. He used to go away on three- or four-day cruises, always after consulting his accomplices, but never once did he cross the Channel in order to take the drugs on board in a foreign port. Instead, he would sail about eight or ten miles from the English coast and await the arrival of certain of his confederates who hired a French fishing-boat for that purpose. Usually Dawkins and The Grubber were the leading lights in that part of the business; and although they had some hazy idea of when Gunville had the "snow", as the drug was called in his circle, they were never certain on that point.

It was Gunville's fertile brain that had decided upon the hollow boom hiding-place. Spars of that description are quite common in racing yachts, when the tendency is to make them a "flattened oval" in section.

On one of his latest adventures Gunville had a row with the fellows in the hired French smack. They said he'd double-crossed them. Perhaps he had. At any rate, they "parted brass rags", and although the *Nut's* owner did not know it, Dawkins and The Grubber swore to get even with him.

This they did, more or less, by knocking him senseless; not on the harbour pier at

Otherport, as the victim had so decidedly declared, but at the entrance to the dark alley, whence he had been carried back to the landing-stage by his assailants. They knew perfectly well that Tarrant Gunville couldn't give the police the true facts without giving away his part as director of operations of this particular dope-smuggling gang.

But slugging Gunville didn't get them very far, from a monetary point of view. They had designs upon the hidden store of drugs on board the *Nut*, and they might have discovered it—that was why they had begun to unlace the sail-cover—when Nick gave them the scare of their lives and a painful nip for The Grubber in addition!

Foiled in this attempt, the two rascals determined to have another try. They knew that the *Nut* was being sent from Otherport to Easthaven with a Sea Scout crew; but they hadn't any idea that a Scoutmaster was forming one of the party.

Here was a chance to intercept the yacht, compel the youngsters to leave her—they would be set ashore on some unfrequented part of the coast under cover of darkness—ransack the *Nut* at their leisure until they found the illicit cargo, and then send her to the bottom without a trace.

It would be quite a simple business. Four or five additional members of the gang would make up a sufficient number to man a couple of motor boats. Their knowledge of the district told them that there were unattended motor craft lying at Dockingham that could be used for the purpose without their owners' knowledge, until they were found either drifting without anyone on board, or high and dry on the beach.

The strangest part of the " peaching " business was that Dawkins's and The Grubber's denunciation of Tarrant Gunville did not end there. The police, after giving them due warning, had obtained each man's story separately, and not in the presence of the other. Dawkins thought he would get off by turning Queen's evidence, and Gubbins was inspired by similar motives. Consequently when the Assizes came off, these two worthies had not only completed the chain of evidence against Gunville but had deeply implicated themselves.

Gunville had given Dawkins and The Grubber away, and they had retaliated. That was not all.

Plausible to the point of recklessness—witness his ready promise to send a cheque to the Princess Margaret Hospital at Otherport—the slimy and pestiferous Gunville (to quote the words of the efficient Mr. Badger) went further. In a futile effort to save his own head or at least to mitigate the force of the blow that was to descend upon it, he gave away his two pals, who at great risk to themselves had put off to the *Nut*, when she was lying off Easthaven, with the invitation to tow her to her moorings, when the dope could have been taken ashore had the Water Guard not taken possession of her first.

Ron Bradley had to give evidence at the trial, in spite of well-meaning efforts to have him excused. Group Scoutmaster Miles was the only other witness from the Sea Scout crew of the *Nut*.

The result of the trial was that Tarrant Gunville was given a sentence of five years and his accomplices proportionate terms of imprisonment. According to custom, the *Nut* was to be sold to help defray the cost of the prosecution.

The Sea Scouts were thanked in Court for the part they had played in the detection of the crime, and, in addition to their expenses, were given the sum of fifty pounds as their proportionate *per centum* of the value of the contraband goods.

That brought them a good deal nearer to the realization of their dream of acquiring a sea-going cruiser.

That was not all.

Their tide of good fortune continued to flow.

It was the chief officer of the Water Guard who pushed matters a bit further when he had a quiet talk with Mr. Miles and Ron soon after Tarrant Gunville had faded out of the picture for five years or less—according to the remission of the sentence gained by good-conduct marks.

" A nod's as good as a wink to a blind horse," remarked the Customs officer. " Let me put you up to a tip. The *Nut* will be up for sale shortly, by sealed tender, and the highest or any offer may not necessarily be accepted. It's the end of the season, and there won't be many prospective buyers. If you're keen, try a bid of one hundred pounds!"

It was well towards the middle of October when the Otherport Sea Scouts received information that their offer had been accepted, and all that remained, apparently, was to pay the money and take over the yacht.

There were difficulties. It was too risky,

now that the delayed equinoctial gales were due, to sail the little yacht to Otherport; so Mr. Dyson, now recovered from his illness, with Ron and Ned, went by train to Easthaven to arrange for the *Nut* to be hauled up for the winter at Bickerdyke's boat-yard.

Wise in their generation, they weren't going to take the yacht there before coming to terms for her storage. They'd drive a bargain first and then bring the *Nut* to the yard.

"Good afternoon!" exclaimed Mr. Bickerdyke, recognizing the Patrol-leader and his chum. "What can I do for you?"

"We—that's the Otherport Sea Scouts—have bought the *Nut*," explained Ron.

"Aye, I know that," rejoined the boat-yard proprietor. "And I know there's someone else who's sorry he didn't get her, and that's Mr. Walsh who owns the *Dark Secret*. I reckon he'd like to have a word or two with you. There he is, over against his craft."

"We came to ask how much you'd charge for laying up the *Nut*," explained Mr. Dyson.

Mr. Bickerdyke smiled.

"We'll go into that after you've seen Mr. Walsh!" he replied enigmatically. "Maybe it'll be to your mutual advantage."

Rather mystified, for they thought that the *Dark Secret's* owner wanted to congratulate them in a sporty manner on their new purchase, Mr. Dyson and the two Sea Scouts made their way between piles of junk and hauled-up boats to the shed where Peter Walsh was busily applying a coat of black varnish to his craft.

" You wanted to see us, so Mr. Bickerdyke told us," began Ron. " This is Mr. Dyson, our S.M."

" Pleased to meet you," rejoined Mr. Walsh. " Can't shake hands: look at mine! Never could slap on black varnish if I'm wearing gloves. But that's neither here nor there. To come straight to the point: what about a swop?"

" A swop?"

" Yes! The *Nut's* a nice little craft, but she's too small for your crowd; the *Dark Secret's* too big for me to handle unless I have some pals with me, and I can never get hold of them when I want them. I reckon I can sail the *Nut* all right single-handed. So what about it? The *Dark Secret* isn't much to look at, though she's sound. She'll stand any survey and her engine's as reliable as one can wish for."

Ron and Ned looked inquiringly at their Scoutmaster. Mr. Walsh had spoken words of wisdom, for, in spite of her weatherliness and handiness, the *Nut*, not belying her name, was not large enough to accommodate even one patrol. The *Dark Secret* had room and to spare for double that number.

" We might consider it," replied Mr. Dyson

guardedly. " She'll want painting, and Easthaven is a long way from Otherport. We can't send a party of Sea Scouts to fit her out. And, of course, there may be defects that neither you nor we know of. She may be soft in places."

" There's not a patch of dry rot anywhere," declared her owner. " I'll tell you what: have her properly surveyed. If she passes that—as I know she will—and you agree to a fair swop, I'll guarantee to deliver her afloat in Otherport Harbour by the first of November, and, what's more, the *Nut* won't be mine until the *Dark Secret* is handed over to you at Otherport."

" I'd like to have a look over her," suggested Mr. Dyson.

" With pleasure. She's been painted inside since you two were here last," announced Mr. Walsh. " She's all dry inside; all you have to look out for is not to get that black varnish on your bare knees!"

Peter Walsh had put in a good deal of useful work during the last two months. Mr. Dyson, who hadn't seen her before, was favourably impressed by the beam and headroom and the " layout " generally. If the surveyor's verdict was what he hoped for, the " swop " would certainly be in the Sea Scouts' favour and quite possibly in Peter Walsh's too.

Then another doubt arose in his mind. All

boats cost something to maintain, and as a general rule the upkeep rises proportionately to the size of the craft. The *Dark Secret*, just under forty feet in length, would require a yearly outlay of at least three times that of the *Nut*, which was ten feet shorter. Most of the labour would be done by the Sea Scouts themselves; but there was the cost of material to be considered. An ill-kept, roughly painted motor cruiser would bring discredit on the Troop; and no Sea Scout acting up to the traditions of Scouting would go round cadging paint and gear! On the other hand, there were yachtsmen and others interested in Scouts who gave, without being asked, various useful things to Troops in the district, and goodness knows, these were fully appreciated.

Unfortunately, Mr. Dyson reflected, there weren't any such benefactors in the Otherport district; or if there were, they hadn't come forward to help, and although the Seagulls had reaped a good monetary reward for helping to lay the dope gang by the heels, it was much too sanguine to hope for similar slices of luck!

But Mr. Dyson had faith in his Troop. He knew that every one of them would work hard to add to the funds. If they failed, he reflected, they would have to dispose of the *Dark Secret*; but from what he knew of them, that wasn't likely to happen.

"Very well, then, Mr. Walsh," he decided. "It's a deal!"

This time the two men shook hands. The fact that a film of black varnish was transferred to the Scoutmaster's hand didn't signify!

. . . .

A fortnight later the *Dark Secret* was lying on her new moorings in Otherport Harbour, with the green burgee with its yellow fleur-de-lys floating proudly in the breeze.

The Otherport Sea Scouts had achieved their ambition!